Waters Like the Sky

Waters Like the Sky

Book 1
The Chronicles of an Unlikely Voyageur

Agnes Rajala and Nikki Rajala

NORTH STAR PRESS OF ST. CLOUD, INC.
St. Cloud, Minnesota

Printed in the United States of America

Published by
North Star Press of St. Cloud, Inc.
P.O. Box 451
St. Cloud, Minnesota 56302

northstarpress.com

◇◇◇ **1** ◇◇◇

CLOSING THE HEAVY DOOR of Father Goiffon's house behind him, André squared his shoulders, prepared to set off toward his home. The familiar quiver of nervousness sent a chill down his back as he peered through the gathering dusk at the path ahead.

Good! I'm glad it's late.

That meant his usual tormentors—Michel, Pierre, Claude, and the others—would be in their homes, perhaps eating their suppers. They would not be outdoors, to greet him with jeers and taunts.

He cringed as he thought of their sneers. *"Bon-à-rien"*— their name for him meant "good for nothing." It was their way of reminding him that, while they were helping their parents with the many chores of wresting a living from their small farms, André was still in school.

But it's not my fault! André wanted to tell them. *My father won't let me quit school, as you've done. I have asked and asked him to let me stop these lessons, but he won't. And what good will they ever do me? When will I ever use mathematics, or Latin, or fancy words?*

1

Thinking of his troubles, he strode heedlessly, his feet crunching through the icy crust the evening coolness had formed over the melted slush from the day's warmth.

I'll ask again tonight, he decided. *I'll tell him he needs me. I could—*

Splat!

A slushy wet snowball whizzed, just inches from André's head, and struck the tree by the path. He had been so deep in thought he had forgotten to watch for trouble, and here it was. At the woodpile in Michel's yard, two of his former schoolmates stood laughing: Michel and Claude. André's heart plummeted. Claude was bold, and together with Michel, there was no telling what they might do.

I won't run. I won't let them make me run. André clenched his teeth and walked straight ahead, not looking around. If only he could get past their yard before something worse happened.

"Oh, look, it's Bon-à-rien! How prettily you walk, Bon-à-rien! Did you learn some new dance steps today? Tra-la-la!" And Michel trilled a silly tune, whirling about with a hand on his hip and the other held over his head.

André made a mask of his face and lengthened his stride. How had they learned about that?

"Are you thirsty, Bon-à-rien, after all that hard work copying verses? Such a nice script you write. Oh, poor Bon-à-rien! Here, have some ice water!"

Splat!

This time the mushy snowball splashed against his neck. Driblets of ice and water ran down his back, while the dirty snow slid down his coat, leaving a muddy smear. André ground his teeth

2

at the jeering laughs when it found its mark. He would not brush it off.

They had come out of the yard, now, and were waiting at the path just ahead.

"Here, have some more," and Claude squashed a handful of muddy slush against André's face.

Michel yanked off his cap. "You mustn't cover up that fiery hair!" he cried, and tossed the cap into the ice-rimmed puddle.

André turned, his arm drawn back to hit—but Michel grabbed it, winding his foot around André's leg and pushing. André fell headlong into the dirt and slush of the path. In a trice Claude was on his back, pummeling him and holding his face into the dirt and muck. André opened his mouth to yell, and had it filled with wet snow.

The two boys rolled together in the icy mud, flailing and clawing at one another, while Michel stood ready, with his hands full of snow. André dug his fingernails into Claude's neck, and he felt Claude's fist smash against his cheek. He pounded Claude's face with his other fist while Claude grabbed his hair and banged his head into the puddle.

At that moment the door of the cottage opened, sending out an oblong of yellow light, and a man's voice shouted, "Michel! What are you about? Get in here with that wood!"

Without a word, Michel turned and went back to the woodpile. Claude got to his feet and slouched off toward his own home.

Shaking, André stumbled to his feet. With fumbling hands he brushed off what snow and mud he could, and continued on his way home, not stopping to try to find his cap. His breath came in big sobs.

That does it, he thought. *After this, Papa will have to let me quit these special lessons with the priest. Why do I need them, anyway? I can already read and write. That's more than my Papa Joseph or Mama Berthe ever learned to do. I write long sentences, very neatly. I read Father Goiffon's books, hardly missing a word. And I can multiply and divide. What for? I should be done with this special schooling. There is no need for the lessons.*

And he was ashamed to keep on at lessons when his parents could use his help. Like the other boys.

But—he had to admit: some lessons were exciting. The history, now—his blood raced at the tales of brave explorers such as Champlain, who went into unknown dangers, and intrepid captains like LeMoine who captured a British fleet with his one small ship. Arithmetic was fun, too, like solving puzzles.

And fencing—ah, that was truly a delight. He thought of Father Goiffon, with his priest's black cassock tucked up, shouting *"En garde!"* and thrusting with the sword-like wooden stick he called a foil or an *épée.* André would do his best to parry the thrust of the priest's *épée,* dancing backward and then slipping forward. All the while Father Goiffon would be calling instructions: "The wrist, the wrist! Watch for the opening. Now thrust!"

André knew he was gaining more skill every day. Once or twice he had managed to get under his teacher's guard, thrusting his *épée* into the priest's broad belly. And, today he had almost managed to knock the foil from the good Father Goiffon's hand!

André's eyes glowed at the thought.

Yes, he did enjoy some of the lessons. But, all the same, it was wrong. He should not be whiling away time at such things when his parents worked. Lately it had seemed Papa's shoulder

4

bothered him more. Many evenings Mama had rubbed it with the oil that had such a pleasant smell.

If I were at home, I could do some of the chopping and lifting that caused Papa pain. Even last winter it had been better. Then, if Joseph was not hurting on cold or rainy days when outdoor work was impossible, he had entertained them with magic tricks.

"You see this rope?" he would say. "Just a plain rope. See, I pull it straight out. No knots. Now I do my magic on it— *abracadabra*. And look! Oh, my, what has happened?"

Papa would shake his head, looking helplessly puzzled as he held out to André two pieces of rope—surely it was the same rope, but how had it become cut?

"Now what?" he would say. "Do you suppose I did something wrong? Let me try again." And he would solemnly perform another magical act, and the rope would be whole again.

Other times he would make things disappear. Moments later they would find them again, in impossible places. For years, no matter how closely André watched, he could not see how it was done. Neither could Mama. She would cluck in exasperation when her darning egg—which she was sure was in her knitting basket— would suddenly be found in her pocket. Joseph would laugh at her amazed look when playing cards were pulled out of her apron, or a potato came out of her ear.

In the cold months of winter, André had finally learned how to do some of the tricks that were so mysterious when Joseph did them. Now he could pluck a spoon out of the air, or extract a ball of yarn from Berthe's hair.

He had liked showing the tricks to the others at school. The boys had all been friends, once—but not now.

Well, they wouldn't sneer at him any more. He would quit the lessons, even the ones he enjoyed. He would stagger into the cottage under an immense load of wood, he would carry Berthe's wash water. The minute he got into the cottage he would tell his parents what he had decided.

His eyes snapping and jaw firm, he passed the gate and started down the short path to the doorway. Supper would be waiting. Papa would be smoking his pipe by the fire, Mama knitting, and the table laid for the meal. He opened the door.

Something was wrong.

His parents were in their usual places, it was true. But Papa wasn't smoking; Mama wasn't knitting. They sat still, stiff, as if something had frightened them. Their faces showed shock and worry.

◈◈◈ **2** ◈◈◈

SHUT THE DOOR," PAPA SAID, although André had shut it already. He hung his coat on the hook behind the door and came to the fire. He looked from one parent to the other. Something had happened—but what?

His father spoke. "We have had—a letter."

A letter! This was strange indeed. As far as André could remember, the Didiers had never had a letter. Nor had any of his classmates in the village.

Papa went on, in grave tones. "We have been waiting for you to tell us what it says." He nodded toward the table.

There the letter lay, a square of white, as if he feared to touch it. The blob of red sealing wax bore a fancy crest pressed into it. Hands trembling with excitement, André picked it up, wondering. He put his finger under the seal, to open it. The crisp heavy paper crackled as he unfolded it. On the single page was the same crest embossed with gold. The writing was clear, flowing like the writing Father Goiffon so patiently taught him. He read it aloud.

"'To my nephew, Nicholas Charles Denis Marie Quevillon: You must return to France at once. The *noblesse* have been restored to the rights and privileges they held under the *ancien régime*, the old order. Your grandfather is again in possession of his former estates, and his title as Comte D'Ansereau. Since your father's death in the army, you will be the next *comte*. You must come to your grandfather at once. He needs you to help with the estate. Your people in Ansereau await your return happily, as I do also. I implore you to be careful and beware of those who would seize your rightful place. I promise you my steadfast support and loyalty. Your uncle, Georges Quevillon.'"

André looked from one serious face to the other. "But what has this to do with us? Who is this Quevillon? What does it mean?"

His father took his pipe from the table, looked at it, and thrust it into his pocket. "It means—there is something we must tell you, that you need to know. Now. Tonight."

A whimpering sound came from Mama, quickly stilled. André saw her mouth was working, as if she were ready to cry. He couldn't remember ever seeing his mother cry.

Papa took a deep breath. His voice was heavy, as if it were hard to speak. "It is a long story. I must tell you, first, that you are not our real son. Your name is not André Didier, though you have been called that all your life. It is Quevillon—André Louis Jean Marie Quevillon."

Not their son?

André's breath left him. He looked from his father to his mother, and back again. It didn't make sense! All his life Joseph and Berthe had been his parents. He could not remember ever living

8

anywhere except with them. If he were not their child, where had he come from? Why did this strange name, Quevillon, cause his father's voice to shake? He looked down, puzzled and frightened.

"Perhaps you do not remember, but you have a brother. He is Denis Quevillon."

André sat down. He could not believe what he was hearing.

In a steadier voice, Papa began to explain. "You would know nothing about the troubles in France when you were a baby. From Father Goiffon you've learned how the common people overthrew the king. Many cruel leaders were killed for their wrongs. But some of the people seemed to go crazy. They forgot that others, the nobles, had cared for their problems. They forgot that nobles were bound by the code of *noblesse oblige* and were obliged to help those who were less fortunate. But some wanted to hurt everyone who had power over them. The whole country was upset. I will not talk of those times.

"You were part of the family who lived in the *chateau*, the castle of Ansereau. Your father was a captain serving the king, and died of a fever, the infection of his wound, soon after you were born. Your mother died at your birth. There was only one other child, your brother Denis"—he gestured toward the letter— twelve years older than you. You both lived with your grandfather, the *comte*."

Joseph took his pipe from his pocket, looked at it, returned it to his pocket.

"The times were so bloody that your grandfather feared you were not safe in France. Besides, there was an evil man who had tried to kill your brother and you in a carriage 'accident' so he could inherit the *comte's* wealth. Your grandfather sent for me, Joseph, and my good wife, Berthe. He knew he could trust us."

In the brief silence, André heard himself swallow. A pine branch snapped in the fireplace. Papa continued.

"His plan was to send you to Canada, as if you were ordinary people, to live among other ordinary people. He asked us to go with you as your parents, so no one would suspect who you really were. We were proud to be so trusted. But we were afraid, too—we feared for our lives, and yours, as well. There was so much anger and hatred in the land. We did not even dare to say farewell to old friends, though we knew we would never see them or our old home again."

Joseph paused again, gazing into the fire. André tried to picture in his mind what he was hearing, as he waited, hardly breathing.

"You will not remember the gray day when we gathered in the courtyard of the *chateau* while it was still dark. We were all muffled in cloaks, booted and spurred, ready to ride. I held you on the saddle before me, but Denis could ride by himself. We rode like the wind for the coast. The old *comte* had a ship waiting for us, and we sailed at once.

"I did not draw an easy breath until we reached Quebec. For on that same ship was the very man who wanted to steal your lands. We knew we must not let him see Denis or you, because he would try to harm you."

Berthe shuddered at the memory. Joseph glanced her way and went on.

"You were so small we kept you in our cabin. Luckily Denis was sick on the voyage, so we could keep him hidden. This

10

ruthless man—his name is Basile Roche—did not know you were with us. But he was smart and would search. He would hire spies, people to report to him, about what had happened to you. So we realized he must never find out that you had come to Canada. I have done my best to keep you both safe from him. That is why we have never told anyone, not even Father Goiffon, that you are not our true son. Though he may have his own idea."

"But—what happened to my brother? Did that man find him after all?"

"I have worried about that, I can tell you, for Denis was a lively lad and not one to stay home. If Basile Roche once saw him, he would know him for a Quevillon by his face, and even faster by his hair. The color is like yours, between red and gold. Most people have dark-brown hair. Like ours," he said, lifting the loose hairs by his ear.

"But we had a friend who was a *coureur des bois*. Do you know what that means, *coureur des bois*?"

André knew. "It's a woods runner, a free trapper." He thought of the quick, hardy men who followed this life. How brave they must be!

"Well, this man took Denis with him, into the forests to the north that summer and fall. When he came back, Denis was strong and fearless. He went as a voyageur the next spring, a canoeman with the fur brigades, across the mighty lakes to the vast forests where there are only Indians. He has never returned."

Confused thoughts whirled about in André's brain. It all seemed unbelievable. A brother Denis? An enemy named Basile Roche? His mind buzzed with questions.

"But then—who am I?"

Joseph repeated what he had said before. "You are André Quevillon. You are of noble blood. This is why we have kept you at your lessons, such lessons as are not for ordinary boys. We promised your grandfather we would try to have you taught the skills and graces that befit your place in life.

"I know how hateful you have found it, to be different from other boys. But the lessons were needed. For, if your brother cannot be found, or if he no longer lives, then you must be the one to return to France and become the next Comte D'Arseneau. You must be ready to perform the duties of a nobleman, if your brother cannot."

"France? I don't want to go to France! I want to stay here! Can't I just live here, and be your boy, like always?"

It was too much—to have a grandfather in France, a brother he couldn't remember, an enemy who wanted him dead. He thought again of the letter. "This brother, Denis—he's supposed to go!"

Joseph smiled.

"True. He is the next heir. But first we must tell him about the letter and what has happened."

"How? Is there a way to get word to him? How do we know where he is?"

"We must find him, André. That is the first thing. But it will not be easy."

André thought hard. "If we don't know where he is—is there any way?"

"We must try. We know only that he went to the land at the head of the lakes. But the trackless forests have deep secrets. Many things may have happened. He might have drowned if his

12

canoe was upset. He might have been attacked by wild beasts.
Angry Natives might have killed him, as they did Father Alneau.
He might have become lost, or frozen to death, or starved. Who
knows?"

Joseph stared for a while at the flickering fireplace.

"And we must not forget that the spies of Basile Roche
will have sent him this news. He has most likely been to the far
west, searching. Roche is probably still in Canada. He will have
looked for a chance to steal your inheritance—perhaps encourag-
ing an Indian attack, setting traps or worse. He has already hurt
others to get what he wanted. We must also find out where he is,
so we can be on guard."

"You said Denis went as a voyageur, with the brigades."

"Yes, that's what he did." Joseph's eyes glowed as he
thought of it. "Oh, he made a fine voyageur—I can see him yet!
Slim, straight, strong, with his head up, his face shining in the
sun, his red-gold hair hidden beneath his cap—he looked like you
do now, André. And he could sing the songs of the Loire Valley
with the best of them. Oh! A brave sight it was, the canoes with
the light-hearted men, in their woolen *capotes* and bright sashes! I
was part of it. For that year I was also a voyageur. And a winterer
besides—I earned a plume in my cap! Such an honor but only for
those who have spent a winter in the high country, André. And
there were flags, and songs as we swept out into the water—and
the paddle blades flashed in the sun—oh, it was a great time!"

André's face shone. He could see the big Montreal canoes,
with paddlers along each side, jaunty and swaggering, and the
bowman and steersman in their places. They would all be laughing,
cheerful and spirited as they started their long adventure.

I'd like to be one of them, he thought. *Like my brother. My brother, who never returned.* Where was he now?

Perhaps Joseph also thought of Denis, for he went on. "That is the last time we saw him. I know only that he went to a post in the interior. After that, who knows? It was safer not to ask, to keep his whereabouts a secret. So we have had no word. Maybe he lives. Maybe not."

"Isn't there anyone we could ask? Anyone who might know?"

Joseph got to his feet, his mouth determined. "We will see. I have friends among the voyageurs. If we ask, we may find one who knows something."

He moved to the table.

"This is the right time," he said. "Soon it is spring, the brigades will be forming. Tomorrow we will go to Lachine, and we will ask. But now, we will have supper."

◇◇◇ **3** ◇◇◇

T
O ANDRÉ'S SURPRISE, Papa began their search for Denis the next day, and bade André to come along. André's sober face hid his eagerness as he followed his father (Joseph would always be his father) to the old town of Lachine. His eyes widened at sights so new to him: cobbled streets, many inns near the waterfront, different shops. With wind lifting his hair, he filled his lungs with the smell of water as he trailed his father from inn to tavern to shop. In nearly every one they found companions from Papa's voyageur days. These men welcomed him with back-slapping and merry talk.

André's blood surged as he listened to the tales of narrow escapes, wild adventures, canoe races. Visions of Indians, trappers, and fierce animals made his heart race.

Many spoke of disasters, of friends whose lives were lost. At such times they removed caps, and crossed themselves. André's chest swelled with admiration as he stored the tales in his memory to think of later. Such courage! Such light-hearted zest for action! Plainly, Papa had been as adventurous as any. André longed to hear more. He was almost sorry when Joseph steered the talk toward men who had stayed in the west.

The canoemen seemed to think it a great joke that Joseph was now a farmer.

"*Sacrebleu!*" cried one hardy veteran, throwing his arm about Papa's shoulder. "That is hard to believe. You, the quickest to act, the leader on the long trails! My friend, I have never forgotten that night on Crow Lake—you remember, I am sure! There we sat, you and I and Antoine Felix, smoking our pipes. We could hear men yelling and fighting—the Indian camp was not far. How wild they were from firewater they had begged from the trader. It made them crazy." He wagged his head seriously. "A bad thing, that. Liquor is not good. It pickles all men's brains, makes them insane, turns them into animals."

"That was long ago," Joseph said. "Now I am looking—"

"I tremble yet, when I think of that night! How Running Hawk—a friend, but addled by drink—burst upon us, his tomahawk raised to strike Antoine, whose back was turned. He would have killed him! But you—you leaped to your feet and grappled with him. You took the blow on your shoulder. I still see the blood spurting, as you staggered."

He shivered, remembering. "But you hung on, and wrestled with him until you got his tomahawk, and drove him away."

The voyageur waved his arms, punctuating the story with his gestures.

"You saved Antoine's life, my friend, but at what a cost! Your shoulder was torn wide open. We used all the medicines the fort had. Of course, next day the rum was gone, had done it's damage, and Running Hawk had forgotten everything. When we told him, he was full of remorse. How he loved Antoine and you, his dear friends. But it was a fearful gash—so deep! Does it now trouble you?"

Joseph shrugged. "It has healed. But I do not want to talk of that time. Many men live happily with the tribes, sometimes for years. I am seeking news of one like that. Tell me, have you perhaps heard of a person, young, with hair like this boy has, who has stayed in the upper country north and west of the Lake Superior, *il pays d'en haut?*"

The man shook his head, regretfully. No, he had not heard of such a one. All those he knew were dark-haired. But here was Henri Lamotte—a voyageur with many winters in the far west. Perhaps he would know.

And so it went.

When the talk veered to men who had stayed in the vast wilderness, André's heart went *thump! thump!* wildly. He strained his ears to hear more. Would any of these men recall something that would help find his brother? Most did not, making his spirits drop in disappointment.

But two men had stories to tell, and André's chest nearly burst with excitement as they spoke. Yes, said one, he had seen at the Grand Portage two such men—they traded with the Chippewa Indians in the land known as the "place-with-waters-like-the-sky." No, he did not know what sort of hair they had, but they lived with tribes to the west.

The other man reported that many men from the east— some Bostonais, some Canadiens—gathered near where two great rivers met, the "Father of Waters" and the wide "Minne-Soto," a place not far from waterfalls named for St. Antoine. This was the territory of the fierce Dakota tribe, called Sioux by the traders.

His father spoke no words as André followed him home. Even after they had laid aside their wraps, he seemed lost in thought. It was only when Mama said, "Well?" that he opened his mind.

"It was good that I heard no stories of a young trader's death," he said. "And there are many men out beyond the great lakes. No one can say who. Perhaps he is one of them. But we must find out for ourselves."

She sniffed. "You can't go. How can you paddle all that way, with your shoulder? Who would take you as a voyageur?"

Joseph waited a moment. In the silence André heard his own in-drawn breath. He waited for his father's answer. When it came, he stiffened in surprise.

"André will go."

His heart gave a huge jump.

"But—André? He is only a boy! Who would take him in their crew? And look at him—he is not strong enough to paddle!"

"I'll make him strong enough. And, when the time comes, Antoine Felix will take him."

Antoine Felix! The name was magic. André's eyes grew wide. Antoine Felix, the most admired voyageur of them all, the brigade leader whose canoes were fastest and safest, and always first at the *rendezvous* with least loss of cargo. Only specially picked men served in his crew—Papa had crossed the lakes as a voyageur with him. But would such a man take an untried youth? André's heart almost burst with joy. It would be his dream come true— but could it come true?

No more was said that night, but André snuggled under his bed covers, his head awhirl with excited dreams.

With this golden future, André went eagerly to his lessons. He knew now—he needed to be ready to find his brother. Perhaps Papa had spoken with Father Goiffon, for there seemed to be less reading and more number problems, many of them about furs: how much were four beaver pelts worth? What was the weight of ten muskrat hides? How many ninety-pound packs filled a eighteen-foot canoe? Father Goiffon showed him how to record lists and keep changes straight.

Best of all, they fenced every day. André even practiced on his own, and often surprised the priest with his skill.

Thoughts of the coming days so filled his mind he forgot to dread the the taunts of Claude and the other boys. Now that he had a purpose, their jeers bothered him less. He could walk past them, almost fearlessly. They, finding their jibes had less effect, teased less often, less harshly. Someday I'll show them, he thought. They'll see I'm not just a *bon-à-rien*, a good-for-nothing.

At the same time, Papa started his plan to make André a voyageur. While André knelt in a box, a length of ash shaped into a paddle in his hands, Papa sat facing him with a similar implement. Together they would "paddle." At the same instant, each would throw his paddle forward, dip it into the air, and pull back with a brief tug, as if they were canoeing in water. All the while they sang—the endless verses of *Alouette, En Roulant Ma Boule,* or other voyageur songs. These served to keep them in time.

Sometimes Papa made him count strokes—a voyageur must paddle fifty to sixty strokes to a minute.

André's mind reeled, trying to keep all the directions in his head at once. When he did, Papa nodded: "That's it! Good, good—short, quick and hard. That's the way! And sing! Keep your eyes up, watch the bowman, the *avant*. The rock, there watch it!"

If the paddle scraped the floor, he puffed his cheeks and roared, "No-no-no-no-no! Do not dig! Never dig! Dip, pull and swing. And sing, André. Keep in time with your canoemates!"

Will I ever get it right? André wondered.

Before he had mastered the canoe skills, Papa started another practice. André watched, puzzled, as he tied an enormous bale of goods into a bundle with two "ears" on top for handles. Papa demonstrated how to swing the ungainly package onto his back, anchoring it to a line with a strap around his forehead, and how to walk rapidly, bent against its weight. With a wave of his arm, he told André to carry this mountainous load around the cottage.

"It is not enough to paddle the canoe," Papa said. "There are many places where the canoe can't go—falls, bad rapids, danger spots. Then the canoes are unloaded, and everything—*everything*—is carried around the bad place on men's backs along a portage trail."

Mama had protested: "No-no Joseph! It is too hard, too heavy. André is too young, too slight. A young noble should not—"

"Quiet, woman," Joseph had told her. "Would you have him the laughingstock of the other canoemen? If he could not carry his pack, the others would wonder why he was there. And he must carry not one of these, but two! And he must trot, not walk, on the portages! Some of the carries, or portages, are miles long between the rivers he must follow. They're rocky, filled with tree roots, mud, swamp. There are eighteen such carries before you even reach the Mattawa River."

So André sweated and struggled, finally managing to stagger with the immense load around the cottage. But Papa wasn't satisfied. He must do it again and again, faster and faster, with heavier and heavier loads.

"You will find that carrying two packs at one time is not so hard. But you must balance them just right—like this. Do you feel it?

"You won't be expected to carry the canoe," his father said. "Only the hardiest men do that—but you must shoulder your share of the load, and you must not grouse about it."

Grouse about it? Never! Tough struggle though it was, André felt too happy to grumble. He gritted his teeth and tried harder, cheered by each improvement in strength. All that was to prepare him for the life of a voyageur.

André fell asleep each night tired to the bone. Yet, in spite of aching muscles, he couldn't help smiling. He felt himself growing stronger every day.

Even so, he had moments of doubt. Could he keep up with grown men, day after day, in the punishing work of paddling the canoes and carrying the heavy packs? He trusted his father's promise that he could be a voyageur this very spring—but was it truly possible?

Each day Papa added more lessons to build his strength, his endurance.

Then one morning he followed his father along the track that led to the waterfront of Lachine. A light snow had fallen the night before, making the ground firm under their feet in shady spots, while their steps sank into the soft, mushy surface elsewhere. Spring was really coming. André would have liked to walk more slowly, taking time to look about him at the busy scene on all sides. But Joseph marched steadily on.

They passed men inspecting canoes, the large Montreal canoes, the *canots de maître,* that looked so enormous lying here, yet floated as lightly as an autumn leaf on the water. Men stood in knots, talking, white clay pipes in their mouths. Their hands gestured constantly. Nearly all were dressed in woolen *capotes,* or coats, tied with bright sashes. Colorful caps angled jauntily on their heads, some with feathery plumes.

André stumbled along in Joseph's wake, unable to turn his head fast enough to see all the fascinating sights. He almost trod on his father's heel when he suddenly stopped. They were standing before a man dressed, as the others were, in voyageur clothes. In size he was much like Joseph, not tall, but with wide, strong shoulders and a solid body. He had dark, spiky hair. Merry eyes sparkled above a fearsome black beard.

André watched as Papa removed his pipe with a brief *"Comment ça va?* How goes it?"

With a smile of flashing white teeth, the man said, "Joseph, my old friend! How is it with you? Have you now come to join me on my brigade this season?"

Papa shook his head and sighed.

"But no, though how I wish I could say yes! Alas, that arm that met up with Running Hawk's tomahawk will never again be what it was. I can do my work, but never again can I be a voyageur. No, my old friend, Antoine. I have not come with such a thing on my mind."

Antoine! *Antoine?*

Could this be the great Antoine Felix? For a moment André could not breathe, then a big breath made his chest tight. Antoine Felix, of whom André had heard countless tales by the fireside on winter nights! Antoine Felix, the bravest, the hardiest of voyageurs! The most skillful, most daring, the leader all men of the canoes looked up to, who had led brigade after brigade safely through the wildest of rivers and most treacherous of lakes! His mind scurried like a squirrel in a cage as he recalled Papa's old stories of his voyageur adventures.

The two men talked so rapidly André could hardly take it in. He saw, now, a different man than the sober, busy Papa he was used to. Could this be his father, the husband of Berthe, this laughing man who spoke of reckless adventures shared with the famous Antoine Felix?

He felt his father's hand on his back, urging him forward.

"This is my son, Antoine. You have not seen him since he was a baby. It must be all of twelve years ago."

The bright dark eyes quickly inspected André from his head to his heels. The black head wagged sadly. "Bad weeds grow fast," he intoned dolefully, but his eyes danced with mischief.

To André's surprise a quick answering smile lit Joseph's face. "Oh, he is not quite the worst boy. Very hard to look at, of course. But not all can be as handsome as you or I."

"Alas, that's true," Antoine said sorrowfully, while his beard hid a smile. Both men smoked in silence.

"You're making up your brigade?" Joseph said after a while.

"Oho, I have it already. Me, I have no need to wait until others have had their pick. They come to me while the snow is yet

23

deep, and they ask me, 'Antoine Felix, choose me for your crew this season.' And I say yes, or no, or maybe—and still more men come, when my brigade is already filled. No, my old friend, I do not lose sleep over that, me. No, I just look at my basket, here— will it carry me another season, eh?" He gave the huge canoe a friendly pat.

Another pause filled with silent smoking, while André fidgeted, shuffling his cold feet.

"My boy, here, he grows tall. It's time he should go, this year. Beyond the Grand Portage, to *il pays d'en haut,* to the deep woodlands far beyond, to . . . who knows where? But he must go. There are reasons. So myself, I said, I must see my old friend Antoine Felix, to ask if he can find him a place in his canoe."

Oh, the shrewdness, the understanding in those black eyes! Again they swept André, and turned back to Joseph.

"Ah, my friend Joseph! For you I would like to do this thing. I owe you—so much I owe you, my life, even. But I owe my masters, too. How can I say to them, I will not be first at Grand Portage this year? I have taken into my brigade a stripling. He cannot paddle stroke-for-stroke with grown men, he cannot live as they do on a handful of pease. For you I would do this, anyway. I would say to my masters, 'So, I am late. Antoine Felix is not first at the carries, others pass me by, but what matter?'

"But think, Joseph. How can he endure the life? How will he fare with older men who are all strong, tough, uncaring? Who will shield him in the canoe, in the storms, the upsets, the nights when wind and rain cut through him like a knife? No, no, Joseph—life in my canoe is too hard for a young lad. What if I must come back to you and say—he is lost, overboard in the

24

rapids, shot by a warrior's arrow, died of sickness. Joseph, my friend, how can I say no to you? But, I cannot say yes."

He shook his head, his unhappy look showing even through his beard. "But I will help you. Me, I will go with you to other crews, who have untried young men, and I will say, 'If you will take this lad with you, I will remember.' So we find someone who says yes to Antoine Felix. Someone who will bring him back to you, safe." He clapped Joseph on the shoulder. "Come, now, and I will ask."

Joseph did not move.

"I have told you," he said. "He must go, and not come back this season. And more—he must not be noted by any who might be watching. Brigades with boys, with new canoemen— they will be watched by those who search for him, and they would quickly find him. It was my thought that in the brigade of Antoine Felix, no one would think to look. So I have asked this. But—we will say no more about it. What cannot be, cannot be." He shrugged. "Perhaps he will not go, after all. It may be best."

André's heart dropped to his boots. He held his face stiff so no one would know his dream had died, remaining still while the men smoked. The talk turned to other subjects—the weather, the crops, their families. It circled back to the water levels, the upcoming voyages.

"You are a winterer, so I hear. A trader. Antoine, is it not so?"

"Ah, yes. Me, I have been a trader two seasons, now. For me, it is the only life. I love the forest, the trails, the Indian people, the game of furs. Yes, I go this year to build a post where there is no other white man. Ah, the adventure! And it pays well, too. I, Antoine Felix, will be a rich man soon."

"A grand adventure, that. I have dreamed of it, too—where a man lives only if he is strong, and skillful, and watchful every waking moment. It is a good life for you, Antoine. But it is not the life for me, though I envy you. The wooded trails, the game of furs—that I would enjoy. But are there not duties, too? Records, accounts? No, I think those chores would be too hard for me. I do not think it can be great sport for my old friend Antoine, either. I recall he did not love his book, when we were boys."

Antoine sighed. "Yes, it is true. Me, I can write my name and a little more, but to keep track is, oh, very hard. Many hours I spend, and much sweating, to make it come right. And then the *commis,* who keeps the records, he says I make a mistake." He shook his head. "Much I wish I had kept that nose of mine in my book just a little, little bit more. Then I would be able to answer the *commis.*"

Joseph puffed for a moment. "Yes, one is wise too late. A boy thinks only of fun, of doing things outdoors. He does not wish for learning until he is older. Our fathers did not know. They should have done as I have with this boy of mine. I make sure that he goes for schooling, all these years.

"Did I tell you he can read? Whole books, even. And he writes like a priest. Any word he can put down, so that the paper talks. And cipher—why, he can count bales so fast, he says the sum before I've counted all the pelts! And he knows what it is in money, and keeps it all separate, too." He shook his head, marveling, "but he is like all boys. Do you think it makes him happy? No, he would rather be in the woods, following trails. Well, I must go now. Spring is coming. I have much to do. *Bonjour,* my good Antoine."

As André followed his father away from the canoe landing, his feet dragged. He had not truly expected to join Antoine Felix's company of voyageurs. All the same, a tiny spark of hope had flared like a white flame when he heard his father's request. And the hope, it had died so quickly! He knew he had no right to feel disappointed—how could he expect anything else? But his father had seemed so sure. Now he must wait another year. Another year of being a schoolboy, being jeered at, a good-for-nothing. He plodded along, eyes on the ground.

Suddenly his father cuffed him, hard, on his shoulder. He tumbled, sprawling into the melting snow, his head barely missing the edge of an upturned canoe. He lay under it a moment before he could get his breath. Then he got carefully to his feet, dusting the snow off his clothes, and ruefully surveying the wet patches on his knees.

His voice trembled. "Why—why did you do that, Papa?"

Joseph helped him to stand, brushing snow from his back. For a moment he said nothing. Then he gestured toward a man who had just passed on the far side, now disappearing down the trail.

"You see that man? Look at him closely, so you will know him again. That is Basile Roche."

André looked. From the back he could see only the stocking cap. The coat and sash. The man looked much like other voyageurs—stocky, broad of shoulder, with short but strong legs. He walked with a swagger, and carried his shaggy black head as if he cared for nothing—like the dog he kicked that slept too close to the path. Yet something about his burly frame made him repulsive, slovenly. André knew he would remember him.

Papa brushed more snow off André's shoulders and cap. "I am sorry, my boy. But it was necessary. Me, I did not want you to be seen by Basile Roche. He is cunning, and will stop at nothing."

He looked after the man, now nearly out of sight. "This makes me uneasy. Basile Roche must be going in a brigade from Lachine. We must make sure he does not see you, nor hear your name." He puffed for a moment on his clay pipe, thinking.

"But—will there be a brigade that will take me? Antoine Felix will not. How will I be able to go?"

Surely, after hearing what Antoine Felix had said, his father must know his chances were hopeless. But Papa spoke calmly. "Oh, yes. You will go."

He stood for a moment in thought. "But you must hide your hair. We can darken it for a short while. And you will need another name, I see that now. You cannot be Quevillon, nor yet D'Arseneau. Didier is as bad. He will recognize you as the boy I hid. Think, boy. Is there any other name you are called? Or, have you a nickname with your friends? What do other boys call you?"

André gave a short, unhappy laugh. "They call me *Bon-à-rien*. Good for nothing."

But Joseph did not laugh. "It will do," he said. "That is what you will be called. From now on, your name is André Bon-à-rien."

Well, thought André, *after this nothing worse can happen. And now I will have no chance at all of being a voyageur. It's hard enough for a young, untried youth to get into even a poor brigade, but no one will take on a green weakling whose name means "good for nothing." Maybe it's a good thing Basile Roche may be leaving with the brigades. At least he won't be around. But how will Papa manage to send me to the upper country. Not with the brigades, that's plain.*

◈ ◈ ◈ **4** ◈ ◈ ◈

THEN THE IMPOSSIBLE HAPPENED.

André rushed home with news—during sword-fighting lessons he had disarmed Father Goiffon twice, sending his foil flying! In his elation he was inside the door and starting to speak before he saw who sat at the table with his father, drinking tea and eating Berthe's good buttered bread.

It couldn't be!—but it was. There sat Antoine Felix, his eyes sparkling as ever, talking with Joseph of the weather, the news of the parish, all the unimportant happenings that made up their lives. André managed to speak respectfully before taking himself off to a corner by the fireplace. He listened quietly as was good manners for a young person in the presence of his elders.

They spoke of the preparations for voyageur brigades, which would soon be leaving. André ducked his head to hide his hopeful grin as he heard their visitor say, in a careless, offhand way, his eyes very round and innocent:

"I must tell you, my old friend, of a very good new idea I have had. I am a very clever fellow, me. I have been thinking—

29

why should I not take with me into the upper country a *commis* of my own, a clerk to write and figure for me? Oh, not like the *commis* the factor has—there would be no need for so many records. But, do you not think there might be some lad who longs for the adventure of going with the brigades? And such a lad might even wish to spend time in the deep forests—perhaps even a year, say. He could help build the post, would learn the ways of our Indian brothers, how to trade for furs—do you see."

Antoine's face looked sober but a spark of mischief danced in the black eyes. "Me, I think I have been very clever to think of such a good idea. I wonder how I ever came to think of it," he said. "I cannot imagine what put it into my head."

Joseph looked equally serious for a moment. Then the two men burst into laughter, grasped each other's hands across the table, and thumped each other on the back.

"Joseph, my friend, you are an old fox! So now you will have your wish. This stripling of yours shall be with my brigade, if he still wants to go."

If he still wanted to go! André held his breath again.

"But of course," Joseph said. "In which canoe will he go?"

"Mine. The lead canoe."

"You know, of course, that he is untried. You will watch over him?"

"You have said that you want no one to notice him. If he is seen as favored, do you think that will not be marked? No, old schemer. I will treat him just as I would any other canoeman. But, I assure you, he will be all the better for that. And he will come to no harm, I promise. When he comes back, you will see—he will be a man. A man of the north."

They talked then of his "engagement," when the canoes would leave, what André needed for his "outfit." André listened hard—it was for *him* they were making such plans.

But dizzying thoughts whirled in his head. To go in the brigade of Antoine Felix himself! And in the lead canoe!—and why? Because he could read, write, and do sums! Oh, how crafty of Papa to tell his old friend about André's skills! Antoine had taken the bait—thinking it over. He saw the benefits of having his own *commis* to keep his accounts, especially one who wanted to winter in the upper country! So now André had a place in his brigade, and at the post in the wilderness, too. Oh, the delight of it all! André vowed to practice the carrying and paddling until he was as good as any voyageur. He would show Antoine Felix that he, André Bon-à-rien, could be depended on!

Of course, a true *commis* kept many more records than André would need for Antoine. Still, he couldn't keep back his smiles. Just think—he would be spending the winter in the forest, learning the ways of the fur trade. Excitement bubbled inside him, making him almost breathless. Perhaps Antoine Felix would give him other tasks, like going among the Indians, those dark-bronze people he'd never seen. Above all, he would be able to hear of any man of the north who might be his lost brother. At that thought he sobered. If Denis still lived, here lay his chance to find him.

No wonder Papa wore a triumphant smile. Knowing that Antoine could not accept a first-time canoeman in a brigade with his seasoned veterans, the refusal was no surprise. But a *commis*—that was different. Often they, like the factors, the partners of the fur companies, went in the canoes as passengers, and did not lift a finger to help. In fact, they were waited upon, carried to shore on the backs of the voyageurs.

So he had planted the idea by offering André as a boatman, one who would stay over winter. Then, wisely playing on Antoine's dislike of paper work, he had shown a way out. He had counted on his friend's offer.

The last weeks of April whirled by in a frenzy of preparation. Standing straight, with shining eyes he signed *André Bon-à-rien* to his engagement contract. Proudly he accepted a blanket, tobacco, a third of his wages, and the items that made up the voyageur's outfit, which marked him as a voyageur. It was hard not to swagger as he handed the money and tobacco to his parents, and watched others who could not write sign "X." On his return, he would have more than twice the amount for Joseph and Berthe.

At home they got ready in other ways. Berthe's nimble fingers produced a striped voyageur's cap with tassel, and a flashy red sash. Needles and thread, cup and spoon, a few coins, and other things were gathered into his bag of "possibles"—but only those items truly necessary, because cargo space in the canoes was for trade goods, not personal gear.

Both Maman and Papa constantly bombarded André with things he might need to know. Berthe kept anxiously showing André plants: "This little plant—see, it has four leaves—it is dogwood, and very good to reduce fever. And this one, trillium, with three leaves, you will recognize easily, and it will relieve pain—both the leaf and the root." André tried to remember them all: balsam for skin problems, witch hazel for sprains, willow bark for headache and other ills, and for upset stomach—what was it, again?

Joseph gave lessons of a different sort. He drew river and land maps in the dirt outside the cottage. "Now, first there is the St. Lawrence. You have known it all your life. It will cause no problem. The Ottawa, next—it is fast, and strong, and is coming downhill, so it has force. It does not want you to pass, so you work hard for every inch. Then the Mattawa, smaller, with water the color of tea. You still have to fight the current. And in so many days, you will reach . . ."

The magic names swirled like music through André's mind, as he stored them in his memory: Nipissing, Michilimackinac, Isle Royale, Grand Portage. "You will not be asked this, my son—Antoine knows every carry, every rapids, the whole route. But it helps to know what may come."

Even the vast wilderness was part of the magic. "Waters Like the Sky," André murmured.

"What?" Joseph asked.

"Voyageur country . . . Waters Like the Sky."

Joseph smiled. "Well, the Sioux have a word that translates to 'sky-tinted waters,' which is much the same."

There were warnings, too, about Basile Roche. "I fear he knows what happens in France. Perhaps he too has received word that the *Comte's* lands are safe again. He will scheme to stop Denis and you in order to claim the riches for himself. You must be watchful, my son, for he is as cunning as he is merciless."

Though his head buzzed, André tried hard to remember everything. Who knew what he would need, when the time came?

April flew past, followed by May. And then—the great day came at last.

André's very skin tingled with excitement mixed with awe as he looked about him. He was here, actually here, at Lachine! He had hardly time to breathe, taking in the surprising sights on all sides of him. There in front, tethered to the shore, ranged the big Montreal canoes, at least thirty of them, with brightly painted bows showing eagles, deer, stars! Flags adorned every prow. Men were stowing an impossible number of wooden boxes, kegs, and canvas bales in each one. The waterfront seemed alive as men milled about, hurrying in every direction—clerks with papers and small boxes, voyageurs in their colorful costumes, well-wishers come to see the daring men set out for unknown dangers. Everyone seemed to be talking, waving arms, laughing. Noise, happy noise, filled the air. André felt goose bumps on his arms as the excitement built in his heart.

Friends gathered near some voyageurs to see them off, but André stood alone. Papa and Maman wanted to come, André knew—but Papa shook his head. No, it would not be wise. If Basile Roche happened to be at the wharf—perhaps even embarking in a canoe—nothing must make him aware of André. And André must cover his head, for who knew where Basile might be? Pride mixed with sadness in their farewells. A big knot of homesickness gathered in André's stomach as he fingered the knife Joseph had given him as a parting gift—the knife he himself had carried as a voyageur.

He kept as close as he could to the men of his canoe. Antoine seemed to be everywhere, seeing to dozens of small matters that concerned the crews of the four canoes of his brigade. The other canoemen appeared less busy, but one could feel their alert readiness. Emile Felix, brother of Antoine (who would be steersman, though he was perhaps only eighteen years old) stood near, his long paddle in hand. Jean Ducharme and Pierre Manet, both with ostrich plumes in their caps that showed they had wintered in the northwest, talked quietly. André knew they would be paired in the canoe. He wondered who would paddle beside him—surely not René Auger, who looked so squat and powerful. François Laurent or Jacques Comeau, perhaps? He hoped it would not be Paul Doyon, the scarred, ugly-faced, surly-looking man with the twisted nose that seemed to twitch from time to time, and the perpetual scowl. The others called him "Pretty Mouse," a name that surely did not fit, for he looked broad and strong, and certainly not pretty! He didn't hear the names of the last crewmen, no doubt "pork eaters," who went only to Grand Portage and would come back instead of spending the winter.

His smile broadened with a small feeling of secret glee. He would not be a pork eater! And, next time he went from Lachine, he, too, would wear an ostrich plume!

The noise grew louder. There were shouts and shots, and the church bells rang merrily as André took his place with the others of Antoine's lead canoe. His heart seemed to bounce up into his throat when their canoe slipped further out into the water, with Antoine grinning at the bow and Emile standing tall at the stern. Another canoe slid near—and another—until the river was alive with men in birchbark craft, with flags fluttering like bright butterflies and bells clanging. Behind them guns spoke, and the church bells rang even more gaily.

The man called Pierre shouted, "Sing!" and began:
"Alouette, gentile Alouette,
Alouette, je te plumerai"
And in moments the whole river front rang with song, while the shining blades danced in the sun in time, dipping in the

water and swinging out together. There was no time to think of his place—it was beside Pretty Mouse!—as he dipped and swung his paddle, singing lustily, hearing the clamor of the bells and the people on shore.

The canoes swept up the river, the brigade of Antoine Felix in the lead. But they were not truly started. At the westernmost point of Montreal Island stood the church of Ste. Anne, who watched over voyageurs. They must stop, with caps removed, for a brief prayer to ask the saint's protection, and André, like the others, had a coin to put in the offering box. Joseph had prepared him.

Throughout this time, André's feeling of elation stayed with him. The exciting newness of it all—the smooth movement through the water, the gleam of paddles as they flashed through the sun in time, the rollicking songs—passed like a dream. And he was truly part of it!

Nevertheless, uneasiness crept over him as he thought of another of Papa's warnings. He must expect teasing, Papa had said. Voyageurs always teased each other. They made fun of any clumsy move, or chance accident. As the youngest member, and a greenhorn at that, André must watch that he did not let himself be fooled by tall tales, and if he was teased for failures, Papa said he must accept that with good grace.

The St. Lawrence slipped past, and the space between the canoes grew. Antoine's lead canoe, with its picked men, held to the right, sweeping into the fierce Ottawa River without pause in spite of the strong current. And the singing continued.

This was adventure! André's heart thumped crazily as the shore slid past, a blur of green. He paddled stroke-for-stroke with the other canoemen, though he had scant breath for singing, concentrating on holding his own—so far . . .

The moment he dreaded—the first portage—came all too soon. Swift water foaming and tossing around rocks caused a halt. Quickly the men unloaded and beached the canoe. André barely saw as Antoine and others lifted it to their shoulders and disappeared down a trail. The other canoemen matter-of-factly heaved the huge packs to their backs and shoulders, following them. André gritted his teeth and seized a ninety-pound bundle, hoping that the long practices at home would help him now. As he puffed, struggling to swing it into position, he felt René Auger pause beside him.

"Oh, look, my friends! What have we here—is it Samson himself, perhaps? So strong! Look, he has already a bundle. Oh, what muscles! But of course he wants another bundle, maybe two." He clucked, as if amazed. "Here, I will put them on for you." He reached for another pack.

André had not yet settled his first bale when he felt the *thump!* of another, nearly knocking him down. His face reddened with shame and anger. Before he could speak, Emile Felix beside him growled something. Auger dropped the bundle, hefted his own load, and started along the trail.

What was that about? André wondered. What did Emile tell him? Was Antoine Felix protecting him, after all, through his quiet younger brother? Gratitude surged through him as he lurched down the path with his first load of bales.

As Joseph warned, there were many such stops. His arms grew heavy with weariness, a stiff knot of pain lodged itself between his shoulders. He watched enviously as other paddlers seemed to swing their blades without effort, while he found his stroke sometimes going too deep, or feathering the water so that it shot a jet of icy spray.

Beside him, Mouse growled: "Bon-à-rien, do not scoop." And "Bon-à-rien, hold your paddle so." "Bon-à-rien, you need not push so hard, others are paddling too." André tried to mend his stroke, but the mistakes kept recurring.

Soon his arms ached, and his shoulders felt sore at each movement. His legs felt stiff—if only he could move them. He thought he could not endure another moment, but hours of torment followed. When at last the canoes drew into shore for the night, he could hardly unfold himself. He stumbled blindly under the shelter of the overturned craft, his palms a mass of stinging blisters, and his muscles screaming in protest. Others gathered at the fire, eating supper, but the thought of food made him groan. All he wanted was rest. Was he too weak to be a voyageur?

Presently he felt Mouse by his side. He kept his eyes shut. If he seemed to be sleeping, perhaps the other would go away.

No such luck. "Bon-à-rien, here is food. You must eat," Mouse muttered by his ear. He crouched near with a dish of some thick soupy stuff that smelled good even to André's weary nose. He sat up, took the dish and slurped up every drop, wiping the dish with the lump of bannock bread that followed.

Mouse had gone, but soon he was back. "Bon-à-rien, give me your hands." André held out his bloody, stinging hands. Mouse took first one in his great paw, then the other. The soothing comfort of something being smeared on them calmed the open blisters.

"Bear fat," Mouse grunted, spreading a thick coating on the tender palms. It felt like balm. Mouse took a wide strip of something that turned out to be soft leather, winding it around André's wounded hands and binding them tightly. "Wear those tomorrow." he growled. "And, Bon-à-rien, you must move. Yes, move everything that hurts. If you lie still, you will get more stiff and sore. Walk, now, and stretch. Then curl up in your blanket." And he disappeared into the darkness.

Why, he is kind, André thought in a daze. *Perhaps that growling in the canoe was meant to help me. Tomorrow I'll pay more attention—maybe then it will be better.* And with that, he fell asleep.

As it turned out, tomorrow *was* better, though at first his sore muscles pained like fire. He watched Pretty Mouse closely, patterning his strokes with his, which seemed to help. And on the portages, things went better, even when Mouse spoke at his side with a frown and a snarl:

"Why do you walk so, you? Lean—this way. Look at the ground where you put your feet. Then your back will bear the load." Of course—that was what his father had said. How could he have forgotten so soon? It made all the difference.

When at last the second grueling day ended, he ate at the kettle with his mates, feeling hopeful. *Today went better*, he thought. *Tomorrow may go better still. If I just keep on, I may become what I want to be: a true voyageur.*

◇◇◇ **5** ◇◇◇

DAY FOLLOWED DAY, each more thrilling—and more agonizing—than the one before. The canoe glided past banks green with new spring leaves and early flowers. André worked hard at doing what seemed so easy for the other canoemen. Still, he was becoming stronger, he could tell. Soon he felt at home in the rhythm of each day's work. The canoeing no longer brought intense pain, though at night he was too tired to think.

His parents at home seemed far away. How were they faring, he wondered. They would be thinking of him, even as he was missing them. And Denis was almost a dream.

On portages, he could still barely manage two bales, along with carrying in his hands the odd-shaped pieces that didn't fit in the bales. Would he ever be able to trot as his crewmates did? Would he ever be able to carry three?

Almost worse than a portage was a *décharge,* when men guided the half-unloaded canoe through the river by holding ropes, wading beside it in icy water to their waists. Not that anyone ever complained, no matter how frigid or fast the waters.

40

They did whatever Antoine ordered with jokes and good humor, though the jokes stopped when the ever-present danger hovered too close. Then men's faces grew grave, and chatter ceased.

Every day brought new scenes. The crosses on the bank, where there were treacherous falls or rapids, sobered them all. These, Joseph had told him, marked the graves of voyageurs who had lost their lives in the foaming waters. All singing and laughter stopped. André, with the others, bared his head and crossed himself. If the crew knew who had died at this spot, a feeling of sadness and loss would shadow them all. That night, to a quiet, thoughtful audience, one man might relate a tale of how the tragedy had happened. "I saw it," he would say. "I was there. We could do nothing."

They told other stories, too—some true adventure tales, filled with dash and daring. Others were wild tales, often aimed at André, the newest recruit and the butt of many jokes. This he had expected—had not Papa told him? So he smiled with the others when René Auger claimed he could not sleep unless André covered his head, because his bright hair kept René awake. He listened with a straight face when François cautioned him to beware the *croquemitaine,* a bogeyman, who (François said) came sniffing about the campsite on moonlit nights. François urged him to remove all his sweat-stained clothes, and sleep naked, to avoid this dreadful creature, which otherwise would surely seek him out.

"Why just me?" André wanted to know. "Why not you?"

"Oh, I wash my clothes all the time, in the *décharges,"* François explained. And, true, François was always one of the men holding the canoe at such times. "So I do not smell. But you, Bon-à-rien—oh, I fear for you. Once the wild *croquemitaine* gets a whiff of you, he will come. And you will feel him nibble at your hair," (here André felt something lift the hair on his neck) "and your ears—do you feel that touch? But if you pile your clothes far away, you will be safe."

"Of course, the mosquitoes will bother you some," Jacques added. André could imagine the laughter of the men if he behaved as François suggested. Certainly they would be amused at his misery from the mosquitoes. Clouds of the annoying insects swarmed around the campsite each warm night. Though the hardy voyageurs wasted little time swatting, they despised the pests.

"But you mustn't get too far from us," Pierre continued the joke. "You know, the woods are full of Indians. I hear what they would really like is a scalp the color of yours. If I were you I would tie my cap under my chin."

Jean nodded sagely. "I once knew a man with hair almost like yours, but yellower. That is, I knew him for a while. Poor man. He forgot to wear his cap, and, do you know, the thought of that beautiful scalp was too much for one Indian brave. Not long after, I saw that brave, and dangling from his lance was my friend's hair. Tsk-tsk. So sad!"

Of course it wasn't true, André knew—or was it? Did such things really happen? He did not intend to remove and pile his clothes, or tie on his cap, as they suggested. Still, an uneasy feeling crept into his thoughts.

"If an Indian gets you, or the *croquemitaine*, Bon-à-rien, could I have your bag of possibles? And your knife?" This was René. "Perhaps you would like to give it to me now, while you take off your shirt."

Surely they could not all be part of the joke. André's confidence wavered. He started to stand, not sure what he would do next. Then he felt Pretty Mouse's hand on his shirt, holding him still. André let out his breath, and grinned shakily. So, it was a joke.

"Maybe I'll just take my chances," he said, shamefaced. "I will sleep right beside you, and if the *croquemitaine* comes, perhaps you will chase him away."

Then there was Nanniboujou, the Chippewa mischief-maker. Pierre and René urged André most seriously to make offerings to this person (who seemed to be almost a god), lest he suffer some mischance. A bit of tobacco, now, to keep a tree from falling on him on a portage; or a small trinket during a thunderstorm, so that lightning should not strike him—Nanniboujou sometimes tripped those who ignored him. Pierre would deal with Nanniboujou, if André would leave the gift with him. Sometimes, half laughing, the other voyageurs would leave their own offerings to Nanniboujou.

One night after supper he stopped, riveted, at the faint sound of music coming over the water. There it was again, and louder. Was that the *croquemitain?* Nanniboujou? Something worse? His imagination?

Wide-eyed, he turned to ask the question that trembled in his mind, when Jacques spoke: "Aha—I hear Gaspard's fiddle! Now we will play!"—and a spirited dance tune lifted André's heart with its bright melody. He had almost forgotten that other crews were part of their brigade. Their encampment must be close by— the music now came clearly, merry and fast.

At once Jean leaped to his feet, bowing with a flourish before Pierre. In response, Pierre put a hand daintily on his hip, raising the other above his head, and the two whirled off in a lively dance. In no time, François and Louis too were leaping and twirling merrily, while Emile and Pretty Mouse sat laughing and clapping. The revelry went on for some time, much to André's amazement. He had not imagined the hard-working paddlers could enjoy such light-hearted fun.

He thought back over the days he'd lived as a voyageur. Pleasure flowed through him at the memories of otters playing, a deer standing beside the stream, an eagle swooping toward the water and rising with a fish in its talons. Campfire evenings, with the stories of heroism, the games of chance or skill, even the pranks, added zest. Yes, it was hard work, demanding alertness and strength. But there was comradeship, and a warm feeling of doing his share. *This is a good life*, André told himself. *I'm glad to be part of it.*

Berthe, that skilled cook, would be horrified at the food—André grinned to himself, imagining her shudders at the stew they had every evening (a thick soup of peas, with pork), and again in the mornings. On very hard days, they had extra meals, but talked of the *rubbaboo*, the stew made from pemmican, which they would eat later on their voyage. Sometimes they caught fresh fish. Once, when they were encamped for a day, delayed by heavy winds, Emile Felix and Jean Ducharme shot a deer. They signaled the other canoes of the brigade and shared the meat with them, for their canoe was too tightly packed to bring the venison for the next days' meals.

Joseph would be relieved to know they had avoided accidents. Of course it had not been just luck. Antoine's watch - fulness brought them safely through so many hazards. A few close calls gave them pause—François Laurent caught his foot beneath a rock in one *décharge,* slipping beneath the water. He was saved from drowning when Emile swung quickly around and hauled him above the surface. No one had laughed at the thought of adding another cross to the ones already on the bank. Emile himself had been swept downstream in the wild water when the rope he was holding on a *décharge* parted. All had held their breath until the current flung him onto a sand bar near the shore. After much pummeling and rolling, he got groggily to his feet and the trip went on.

Jeers resounded when Pierre Manet lost his footing on a wet portage, and slipped down a bank, falling into the soft mud. They howled with glee as they watched him roll down the hill, grasping uselessly at small bushes, and ending up smeared with mud and leaves. Pierre had limped for many days. Worse, he endured merciless teasing from that time on, being called "dancing master" with mud puddles pointed out to him as places where he might like to wallow.

André, recalling being teased all too readily, did not add his own words. However, Pierre's leg was merely sore, no tragedy had struck, and for that they owed thanks to Ste. Anne.

In spite of this, running a rapids still dismayed André. He held his breath, thrilled and frightened as the canoe dove into foaming, roaring water, missing by scant inches rocks on every side. Everyone sat tensely alert, the challenge of the danger exciting them all. This happened frequently—Antoine's reputation for being first at the *rendezvous*, the great gathering at Grand Portage, meant that he did not avoid risks.

Each time they ran a rapids, André studied its waters. He noticed how the river's current grew fiercer, and its roar louder. The men, too, behaved differently—some grew silent and watchful, others laughed excitedly. All singing ceased. Suddenly huge rocks loomed in the canoe's path. Water dashed against them furiously, spraying in all directions. The current twisted between boulders so close together André feared a canoe could never squeeze between them. Emile stood tense, eyes on the river, while Antoine moved like a darting otter, paddling first on one side, then the other, changing the canoe's path in an instant. The middlemen's paddles rose quickly to shove the frail bark boat away from scraping rocks that could gash open its sides.

At all costs, they must save the canoe from harm. That could mean disaster—they could all drown. Even a small scrape might let water reach their goods, causing delay while the bundles were dried, and a new piece of bark fitted to the tear. So they fought, with courage and gallantry and grim determination, to keep their canoe safe from the rocks that reared so threateningly and unexpectedly.

The passage lasted only moments, with Antoine's paddle flashing like lightning, meeting whatever challenge the river thrust at them. Pierre, just ahead of André, was swift and alert, but André set his jaw and watched his side of the canoe with paddle poised. Fear bubbled in his throat, until they were safely in smooth water again. He could hardly believe that some of the canoemen treated the contest with the rapids as if it were a game.

Game or not, meeting each day's challenges filled André with fierce joy. He knew he was learning from these men, and not just how to meet the river.

◆ ◆ ◆ **6** ◆ ◆ ◆

EVENTS FOLLOWED EACH OTHER so quickly, André lost count of the time. He saw new animals up close. Once a moose with her calf stood in the shallows, flinging droplets of water on them as she raised her head from pulling roots to eat. A young bear stood in a clearing, his front paws on a log as he gazed curiously at the passing canoe. Sometimes Juneberries overhung the water, nearly ripe, so they could grab handfuls as they slid past.

He no longer feared the start of the day, or crawled aching into his blankets at night. Already at Lake Nipissing things had improved. Weather became pleasant.

"Aaaah," Pretty Mouse said, stretching, and rubbing his back. "The 'old woman' has decided to be good to us."

"Old woman?" André asked, looking around.

"The wind, boy. She blows gently, now. See, we put up a sail, and she does the work. We do not paddle. And that is not all: at French River, we will have the current on our side, too." It was true. Now water streamed past their canoe, helping them glide ever westward.

47

But what was this? Puzzled, André watched as Pierre carefully combed his hair and smoothed his beard. Nearby, René wound his colorful sash about his middle, tying it jauntily. Others got out festive caps, brushed their jackets, carefully tied the bands that held their trousers snug below the knees. He looked at Pretty Mouse—even he was rummaging in his bag for a colored kerchief. What was happening?

"We are nearing Michilimackinac," Pretty Mouse growled.

"Do we stop at Michilimackinac? Why?"

"Oh, not you, Bon-à-rien," François grinned, with a teasing look. "We must not let you near the houses. Why, your hair might set them on fire."

"We go so the girls there may get a look at Pretty Mouse," Pierre said. "They are lonesome for him, those girls. Only think how sad it is that they see him only once a year."

"But don't feel bad, Bon-à-rien," François continued. "We will tell them all about you—how your hair lights the campfire, and how it frightens the *loup-garou*, the werewolf, away from us poor shivering ones. They will be, oh, so sad to miss you, when they hear how you used to be such a great tall fellow, until carrying three packs on the portages mashed you down."

"While you wait for us, you may cook *rubbaboo*," Jacques added. "We will be hungry after the girls have admired us and given us firewater and danced with us half the night. Make it a good stout *rubbaboo,* to put the heart back into us."

André grinned back, hiding his disappointment at being left. He knew now that their teasing carried no malice. But, as it happened, he did go to Michilimackinac. After they beached the canoe—first leaping out of it into the water, as they always did, so its bottom did not scrape in the sand—he found himself heading for the village with Antoine, Emile, and Mouse.

He twisted his head from side to side as they walked, trying to see in all directions. The houses, now—they were like the cottages of his own parish, even fenced with white pickets. It must be that the people were French. There were Indians, too—dressed in bright blankets or leather. He knew enough now to tell that they were from several tribes—Ottawas, Hurons, Illinois, Chippewas—and all ages, from capering children to dignified men. Trying to take it all in kept his eyes so busy he almost forgot to dodge the wild dogs that dashed around them, barking and snarling.

Antoine led them past the tents and buildings, past men talking outside houses, past the fort with its wooden palisades. He stopped before a large house.

"This is the home of Charles Chaboillez," he told them. "He's the trader to whom I'm engaged. He'll supply us with what we need for our post. Much of the time he's traveling to posts in his depart - ment, but he's here now. Come, we will visit him—and you, André, take special note of all he says, for you must know what to record."

André's heart gave a great leap of anticipation. His job had begun!

So much happened that evening he felt sure he would remember it always. After the many days of trail fare, everything tasted strange and marvelous. *I must remember all this, to tell Mama: the venison pasty, the carrots, the pudding—and we're eating on real plates!*

He listened carefully as Antoine and the big dark man with the piercing black eyes spoke of trade matters. He wanted to miss nothing. A small shiver shook him as he heard Chaboillez say, with a jerk of the head toward him:

"And the boy?"

"He goes with me to the post. You need not fear that he will be a problem. He is fast becoming a true voyageur."

"He is perhaps of your blood?" Chaboillez said.

"No, not that. He has a purpose—to find a man missing these many years. It may be that you have heard of such a one—with the same hair, but older?"

But Chaboillez shook his head, regretfully. He knew of no such man in the far-flung department he controlled. "In Athabaska, perhaps?" he suggested.

"Ah, well, we shall see. We may learn more at the Grand Portage. If not, we have the whole winter, " Antoine said.

"I will remember," Chaboillez promised.

André's chance to show his worth came as he prepared the list of additional trade goods allotted to Antoine. He wrote in careful script:

> Blankets, 3 points - 3
> Blankets, 4 points - 2
> Tobacco - 6
> Portage collar - 1

And so on. He counted carefully, listing knives, trousers, ribbon, hats, strouds, dressed deerskins, and the many other articles Antoine would receive at Grand Portage. Some items, such as the black silk handkerchiefs, surprised him. As he presented the copy in his best writing to Chaboillez, he hoped he'd done well.

"He is a useful man, this young voyageur of yours," the trader said approvingly. "If he remains in the fur trade, he could have a great future." André's heart swelled at the praise. If only he could continue to be helpful!

The replacement of supplies for the canoemen took little time. From now on, they would eat dried corn instead of dried peas, and Indian pemmican would replace their pork. André painstakingly recorded every transaction. At last there was a job he could do well. Others were better paddlers, but he was useful, too.

The next day's embarkation was less smooth than their usual leave-taking. Many townspeople were there to see them off, and to welcome other incoming canoes. The men, however, were not their usual cheerful selves. Both René and Pretty Mouse stumbled clumsily, and Jacques appeared cross or sick. As they paddled off, they made small attempts to smile and wave. Still, they showed little spirit as they bent to their paddles.

Thinking how different these weary men were from the teasers who used him for amusement, André grinned to himself. But it was not wise to let down his guard.

As soon as they encamped, Pretty Mouse and René and others who had enjoyed the treats of Michilimackinac too well rolled themselves in their blankets in the shelter of the emptied canoe. Pierre, François, and Jacques sat beside the fire, smoking as they swapped stories. André crouched in the shadows, sewing a tear in his shirt, near enough to hear the exciting tales. He thought they did not notice his presence.

Suddenly a terrifying, agonized scream ripped through the stillness, coming from the forest at their back. André shuddered. He thought his hair stood on end. The men at the fire stiffened and looked furtively about.

Pierre spoke, in a half-whisper: "Did you hear that?"

François threw a terrified glance over his shoulder. "It's a *loup-garou*!" he breathed. "A werewolf!"

André wanted to ask, *"Loup-garou?"* but knew his voice would shake.

Pierre went on, his hushed voice trembling. "He sounded close. Do you suppose he will find us?"

The three men huddled closer together, looking about with wide fear-filled eyes. Jacques' voice quivered. "Have you ever seen him? No, not I, either. But—they say he is a giant, all shaggy with dark grayish fur that makes him hard to see. His green eyes glitter in the dark—ooh, those terrible eyes! They paralyze his victim. He is huge, like a bear, with enormous claws that tear, and horrible teeth. And he sneaks up—so softly—a man may be sitting quietly, when pouf! The great claws snatch him, and he is never seen again."

André edged closer. He felt himself shiver. That dreadful cry came again, like someone horribly tormented. He swallowed hard, while a tight band squeezed his chest.

He could picture the creature Jacques described, a hulking shaggy beast with eyes that glowed green in the dark, talons that ripped flesh, great teeth that would snap a bone.

Jacques shuddered, his voice heavy with dread. "It is terrible! He tears his victim apart, and he cannot cry for help— the beast drags him off to his lair, deep in the dark forest. And then," his voice dropped in horror, "sometimes we hear him cry, like now, in agony as the animal gnaws his vitals."

The hair on André's neck lifted, and chills froze down his backbone. He crept closer to the older men. He looked over his shoulder at the dark forest behind him.

François spoke then, sounding frightened but hopeful. "But perhaps he will not bother us three. A man once told me that, one night as he lay shivering with fear, he felt the furry paws on his face. When the creature felt his whiskers, he went on to seek someone younger and more tender. He does not want old bonepiles like us if there is something better."

"That is so," Pierre said. "And it's not just the whiskers he avoids—it's our sweat. So if one has no whiskers, he can make himself safe in the river. He must sit in the water, so the monster cannot smell him. It is the only way."

André waited to hear no more. That horrible menacing cry had been repeated—perhaps the monster was now closer, crouching in the trees that grew so near. Goose bumps tingled on his arms. Quietly he moved toward the bank. Should he? The swirling river flowed dark and cold—would he really be safe there? In that moment he heard a soft growl from the overturned canoe:

"*Bon-à-rien*, I give you up." It was Pretty Mouse. "Have you never heard a lynx?"

In fact, André never had. But now he stopped, feeling a tide of red sweep up his neck and face. Fooled again! Well, at least he had not gone in the river, thanks to Pretty Mouse. How the ones at the fire would have laughed!

He rolled himself in his blanket, and curled up beside his friend. But it was long before he could sleep.

◈◈◈ **7** ◈◈◈

AND NOW THEY ENTERED LAKE SUPERIOR.
He had thought Lake Huron was immense. But the
majestic sweep and power of the great lake before
them made André's mouth feel suddenly dry. They seemed to be
in a trackless ocean, with only small glimpses of land on their
right.

The "Mother of Lakes," Jacques called it. *A stern, fearsome
mother*, André felt. The towering, wind-whipped waves made
crossing even an inlet or bay fraught with danger. He thought the
waves loomed like hills, which their frail canoe must climb. As the
blue-black water lifted their heavily-loaded craft and dropped it,
his stomach lurched. He watched, hardly breathing, as Antoine
skillfully angled the canoe to meet each wave just right. But it was
their last stretch of water. If the big lake did not swallow them,
they would finally land at Grand Portage.

"This is our last challenge," Emile told him. "We must see
what this Mother of Lakes will do. We hope she smiles on us. Alas,
now it seems she wants to throw a tantrum."

The lake did appear angry. Dark clouds hung low over the heaving water, and wind blew in gusts, making whitecaps that foamed on all sides of them. As they battled their way, waves towered above them like mountains. Their birchbark canoe no longer seemed sturdy. It felt frail, about to be smashed by the water's force.

The voyageurs fought grimly while the gale increased and the sky darkened even more. Stiff with tension, André went limp in relief when Antoine headed for the shore, to camp on a rocky point with sheltering pines.

In a wild rush the canoe was unloaded and turned over to cover the goods, with a canvas stretched over for added shelter. They were not quite done when driving rain pelted them. François swore softly.

"A *dégradé!* How long, I wonder?"

Would a *dégradé*, a wait, perhaps for several days, keep them from arriving first at Grand Portage for the *rendezvous*? André stared, transfixed, as waves taller than a standing man dashed against the rocky shore, sending a drenching spray higher than he could reach. Through the mist that lay over the watery world, even the closest island was hidden. At sunset the rain stopped, but the wind continued to toss the water into a frenzied froth. Emile and François took guns and went off into the forest, returning not much later with a small deer. At the same time, Jacques came smiling to André:

"Up, *Bon-à-rien*. Come, now, it's time you helped improve our dinner. And you, Pretty Mouse—just because you are beautiful is no reason to shirk." He led them over the rocks to a small cove. André's mouth dropped open, dazzled. Juneberries—just like at home! They hung in lush clusters from the tips of the small tree branches. In almost no time the three of them had filled their caps.

It was, indeed, a feast.

Their hunger satisfied, they set about the business of preparing the canoe, readying it to meet the stresses of the next days. He saw other campfires along the shore, and knew other crews were doing the same. As the fire died, the men smoked a last pipe and settled for the night. Next day the bales soaked by the rain dried in the warm wind.

By noon the water had calmed, letting them start again.

They met other squalls in the days that followed. Most of these they avoided, staying in the shelter of the small rocky islets that dotted the coast. One day they were blinded by fog so dense they could not see even the closest canoes in the brigade.

That day they made little progress, but on the day following, the lake was glassily smooth. The wind now seemed friendly, making the paddling much more pleasant than when they had been fighting for every foot.

Since on the open lake there were no falls or rapids, no portages delayed them. Rest periods now were short breaks, or "pipes," when the men paused to smoke. To André, their lake passage, at first so frightening with enormous waves and wild storms, was the best time of all. Antoine's good sense and guidance would bring them safely through all dangers. He was sure of it, now. More, he had stopped feeling like a misfit. He was part of the crew, doing his share. He was nearly as strong. His fears left him.

Though he thought often of home, the heavy sick feeling of missing his home no longer hung over André. Now he recalled joyously his life with Berthe and Joseph. He would have so much to tell them! They would be proud of him. And—with Antoine's promised help—he would find Denis and bring him back.

"The 'old woman' must like us," René said when the breeze seemed to be gently pushing them forward. "Some years, we must wait out a *dégradé* one day out of every three."

"You must thank me," François boasted. "I gave her some tobacco. And I told her, 'You must be very nice, now, as we have this special new voyageur with the hair like summer sun, you must make it pleasant for him or he will be sick.'"

I will tell Papa and Mama about this. Just think—next year I won't be a greenhorn on the trip home!—André was musing, when Pierre's shout startled him.

"Hat Point!"—and a cheer went up from all the men.

To his surprise, though it was early in the day, the canoe now steered for land a short distance away. On shore, the men pulled out their festive clothing—caps with feathers, colorful sashes, bright shirts. Hair was cut and combed, beards shaved.

I won't ask what this is all about, André thought. *I won't give François or anybody else a chance to tell me any more wild stories.*

Pretty Mouse took his arm, pointing. "See there? Grand Portage. We'll be there very soon." A huge grin split his bearded face.

André dug out his own striped cap, knotted his bright sash around his waist, tied a vivid blue handkerchief around his neck, making himself as fine as he could. Around him his canoe mates grinned expectantly. Other canoes of the brigade drew up beside them, doing the same things. When all looked their very best, the canoes took to the water again. All four skimmed the water together, paddling in a flotilla, and the air rang with their full-throated song.

Forty robust voices shouted out the rollicking "Three Brave Captains" first, then "The Wolves Have Me Scared" and "The Beautiful Lisette." André poured out his heart in all the favorites as they flew across the blue lake toward a low meadow backed by an imposing hill. That, he knew, was the start of the Grand Portage—the great carrying-place that was nearly nine miles long, uphill past the falls and rapids of the river leading to the interior.

The brigade turned sharply and swept shoreward with a flourish of paddles and waving of caps. In reply came a volley of shots, shouts of welcome, and more singing from the Indians and traders on the beach.

They had made it! They were actually here, at Grand Portage. And their canoes were the first brigade of the year! Their fearful voyage was over!

Elated, unable to stop smiling, André forgot the first great adventure now behind him. There was no time for sad thoughts that soon he would part from most of the canoemen he had come to feel were his friends. He did not even recall that the new challenge—the search for his brother Denis—must begin now.

"Hurrah!" and "Welcome" was shouted from every side. As soon as they set foot onshore they were engulfed in a wild jubilee. The crowd seized them, laughing, yelling, firing muskets. André found he was laughing with them, as he was thumped on the back with such fervor it nearly knocked him down, hugged by a bearded stranger, his arm nearly wrenched from its socket in enthusiastic handshakes, and danced about by a loudly singing well-wisher. Happily, there were plenty of willing helpers to unload the canoes and bring the goods to the storehouses. *Good*, André thought. *That's one chore we won't have to do again— until we have to portage the goods Antoine takes to his post.*

Now the canoemen were free. They could renew acquaintances with their friends among the Nor'westers who had arrived earlier, men in rough clothing who bore themselves with pride. They were the men who had dared the most, paddling from the farthest posts!

There were dealers who sold "high wines," searched out by thirsty voyageurs. He saw Indians, both men and women, with whom others exchanged news or made purchases.

André was free, too, but he had no one to visit. He wandered about, watching the busy clerks counting and recording the huge piles of trade goods, and mountains of furs. He heard music, watched dancing, as the canoemen celebrated their safe passage. Mindful of his father's warning, he wore his cap as he roved, trying to see everything. The festivities continued, with more brigades arriving each day.

Next spring I'll be here, again, but I'll have money! And I'll buy—oh, there were so many things to buy! Moccasins for Maman and Papa, the soft, bead-trimmed ones that felt like clouds on one's feet. Other things—

His mind whirled with ideas as he made his way back to the place where his own crew had overturned their canoe to shelter them. But it was too early—the loud laughter and bursts of song from the celebrating voyageurs would make sleep impossible. Now would be a good time to climb the hill that stood like a tall wooded wall behind the settlement. From there he could view the whole encampment.

The panorama stretched before him across the hilltop. The stockade, with its buildings (he counted sixteen) lay spread about the meadow, with tall palisades enclosing them. On one side of the fort were the jumbled camps of the canoemen from Montreal—how messy they looked—contrasted with the neat rows of the Northmen, on the other side. Tiny people scurried about in all directions, constantly moving, like a village of beetles. Before it all, the great sleeping lake lapped mysteriously, while the music and shouts of song and laughter rose clearly in the crisp air.

Yet, the silence of the forest beckoned. The forest had secrets, though André saw familiar trees. Poplars there were, and oaks, their leaves shiny. A huge willow with many trunks stood near the path, smaller shoots beside it. André looked again—that sapling with the ridged and twisted trunk was surely a diamond willow. Papa had often wished for a diamond willow walking stick, and here was such a branch! He would peel it and send it back with the Montrealers. René would take it, he knew.

His knife cut a straight branch near to the trunk, and made short work of stripping its leaves and twigs. He could do the peeling and smoothing where they were camped.

André started back down the hill, the knobby stick in hand.

As he reached the place where the trail branched, he saw ahead of him two men. They seemed to be arguing as they went down the trail that led to the huts of whiskey-sellers. The larger man held the other's arm, and seemed to be dragging him along against his will. Something about the big man's threatening air struck André's memory, and he looked again. He knew that rolling walk!

His breath came in a *whoosh!* as it struck him—*that man is Basile Roche!* He clapped his hands over his mouth to stop the cry of surprise that had almost come out. Joseph's warning came to him: he must not be seen!

Quickly he turned from the path, plunging into the woods beside it. The underbrush caught at his feet, and the twigs slapped and scratched his face, but he paid no heed. He was panting when he reached the safety of their canoe.

François and Pierre were already there, their open packs spread around them. They were sorting their belongings and repacking them, for they were among the picked men who would take the smaller North canoes into the far posts at Rainy Lake and beyond.

Pierre grinned up at André. "Ah, our good Bon-à-rien. Of course, it is your bedtime. You won't mind if François and I share a pipe? And then we'll tuck you in, and sing you a lullaby, eh? before we go find our poor friend Pretty Mouse."

Calmer now, André sat on his bedroll and began peeling and smoothing the willow.

"I fear it is bedtime for our Mouse, too," François said. "He is a bit too thirsty for his own good. There are men among the voyageurs who will do him harm, for the sake of that pouch of money he carries."

"Ah, that sounds like Basile Roche. You saw him?"

"Roche," François spat. "Always bad things happen when he is around. He is a snake, that one. Any meanness he can do, that he enjoys. He met my cousin Michel on a slippery portage, and tripped him so he fell on the rocks and smashed his arm. And Roche laughed. Michel could hardly paddle for nearly a fortnight."

"We must track down the Mouse, before Roche gets to him. Some day I will give myself the pleasure of wringing that snake's neck," Pierre growled.

"He is worse than a snake. He is a wolverine," François said, fastening the straps of his pack, "because it gives him pleasure to hurt others. It's not enough that he's torn Pretty Mouse's face. He will injure and rob him again, if he can. We had better find our friend while there is yet time." The two men rose and left.

61

André looked after them, his heart pounding furiously. How lucky he had not been seen on the trail! The picture of the two walking men rose in his mind. Basile Roche, yes—but had the other been Pretty Mouse? Was that who it was?

Yes! Pretty Mouse, trying to break the other's grip, no doubt fearful of who had given him his scarred face. Would Pierre and François find him in time? Would they have needed him to point out the place? The man? If only André had been able to tell them what he had seen!

Perhaps he could still catch them. He peered out in the direction they had gone—but they had disappeared. Poor Pretty Mouse, no doubt the worse for drink, but still knowing he needed to escape from Basile. Pretty Mouse had been kind to him, a friend. Something must be done to rescue him, but what? André had no clear idea. Perhaps he could find Pierre and François if he hurried. Would Pretty Mouse and Basile still be on the trail?

Stick in hand, André ran toward the place where he had seen the men. Not François or Pierre, but there were the other two—they had not gone far. He saw Pretty Mouse pull sharply back, pushing at the one who held him. At once Basile's hand snatched at the smaller man's chest, and came back holding a small leather pouch. At his jerk the cord holding it parted. Pretty Mouse gave a cry, from anger or fear or despair, and reached out to seize it back, only to be pushed into the dirt by the cruel arm of his attacker. As André hesitated, Basile raised his cudgel, poised to strike Pretty Mouse's head.

There was no time to think of what to do—that vicious club *must* be stopped before it reached poor helpless Mouse's head! He gripped his stick and ran toward the men, with no plan in his mind of what he might do. His feet made no sound, and he was almost upon them before he was seen.

"*En garde!*" he shouted, holding the stick before him like a sword. Basile whirled, with a growl and a curse, and the blow he had aimed at the fallen man was turned toward André.

All Father Goiffon's patient teaching came to his hand as he thrust his stick forward, not even thinking. He gave a quick parry and thrust—and Basile's heavy club flew from his hand, landing with a thud in the pathway.

Basile withdrew a knife from his boot. With an oath, he sprang at André, face twisted with fury, hands outstretched like claws.

André shoved the stick into Basile's chest and the big man grunted in pain.

His knife dropped to the ground, but Basile knocked André's stick out of his hands, and then retrieved his knife.

André was suddenly drenched in cold sweat—but all at once there were François and Pierre, standing like a wall between them.

"At your old tricks, I see," Pierre sneered. "Bullying those not as strong as you."

The ugly look on Basile's face sent cold shivers down André's back. "I will remember your faces," Basile said. "When you least expect it, I will come for you." For a moment he stood, casting a glowering glare at them all. François and Pierre stood firm. With a muttered curse Basile went off down the road.

André's legs turned to jelly. He sat down, breathing very fast. He was only now realizing how close he had been to being beaten, along with Pretty Mouse.

Pierre began to laugh. "Bon-à-rien, you're a wonder. When I saw you run at him—it was like David and Goliath! A cub attacking a grizzly!"

"His face, when his magic wand went sailing!" François was grinning. "But now, Bon-à-rien, you must have a care. You have made a bad enemy. He will not forget. He will watch for a chance when you are alone, so he can hurt you and get even. Always watch your back, wherever you are."

The two men helped Pretty Mouse to his feet, brushing him off and scolding him.

Pretty Mouse was explaining, "But I did not want to go— he grabbed my arm. he dragged me. He said he wanted to buy me a drink for old times' sake!" he shuddered. "I knew he would trick me to get my money, so I hid some in the woods. But now he has what was in my pouch." He sounded almost tearful.

François and Pierre exchanged a look. "Well, we will see what can be done about that. Take him back to the canoe, Bon-à-rien. And stay there, both of you. Do not go out again, unless we are with you, until Roche has left. We will search him out."

As he led the shaken Mouse back to the canoe, André felt unnerved. At least Basile did not know who he was, but, even so, it would not be safe for him to go about the fort during the rest of this *rendezvous*. He might not be so lucky a second time.

It was much later when the other two returned. They had not found Basile, they said, but would look again in the morning. By this time the other canoemen had come, and the story was told and retold. There was much laughter at Basile's chagrin. Pierre danced about François, who pretended to be Basile, acting out his shame at being bested by a mere lad, while being poked at with a skinny twig.

The laughter was mixed with real concern for Pretty Mouse, and even more for André. René said he would be proud to bring the diamond willow cane to Joseph, and with it the story.

The fear in his heart was mixed with the warm glow he felt at the praise of his comrades. André lay awake far into the night, staring into the darkness and reliving the event.

The morning's search for Basile proved fruitless. It seemed he had escaped with Pretty Mouse's money, after buying such supplies as he wanted for trading with the Indians—whiskey, along with tobacco, knives and guns, François reported in disgust. No one could say where he was—traders believed he had gone with a band of Winnebagoes.

So André was free again to wander about the settlement. He could put the experience behind him.

He was repacking his gear next day when Jacques came and nudged him to his feet. "Up, Bon-à-rien. You are needed. We have business." Mystified, he let himself be escorted by Jacques to a place not far from the encampment, where a small rivulet crossed a clearing before foaming its way into the big lake. There he found his canoemates already assembled, with broad smiles on all faces.

"This is a special ceremony," Pierre announced. He frowned with great seriousness, but his eyes danced. "It is for a special occasion. When a voyageur has slept at the 'height of land,' or embarks for the high country, he becomes a Northman. You have not done that, so far, but you will, when you cross the divide at Fond du Lac, only we will not be with you. After your actions the other night, we feel you are one of us. So we have decided not to wait, we will welcome you into our fellowship now. Stand forth, André Bon-à-rien. We are about to baptize you a true 'Man of the North.'"

Dazed, André felt himself shoved to the front of the group, where Antoine stood grinning, a small cedar branch in his hand.

"André Bon-à-rien, as a Man of the North, I ask you to make these solemn promises," Antoine intoned. In his confusion André hardly heard the promises he made—except that he swore never to kiss the wife of another voyageur against her wishes. That had made them all laugh.

"That is an easy promise to keep," Jean said helpfully. "Especially if they look like Jacques," Jacques poked him in mock anger in response.

Antoine said, "And you promise never to let a new man enter the north country until he has made these same promises, and you have baptized him this same way." He dipped the branch into the stream and sprinkled the droplets on André. Two of the men pointed their guns in the air and fired again and again.

"At the height of land, when we christen new brothers, there is always rum," Pretty Mouse said hopefully. The others laughed.

"Pretty Mouse, will you never learn?" Pierre said. He pulled out a small jug. "Bon-à-rien, you may have the first taste, but only a small spoonful, for it may stop you from growing. The rest of us will finish it." André tasted—something like Berthe's cordial—and passed it on. Each took a sip, and the jug was empty.

Together they walked back to their tent. There was laughter and joking, but André did not hear. His heart was filled with joy.

I am part of this. They have accepted me. They may call me Bon-à-rien, but they believe I am good for something.

He thought he had never been happier.

◇◇◇ **8** ◇◇◇

THE NEXT DAYS PASSED IN A BLUR. There were leave-takings as the men bound for far-flung posts started up the nearly nine-mile carry that gave Grand Portage its name, and the "pork-eaters" started back to Montreal with the great canoes, this time laden with furs.

André was busy with the clerks in the stockade, recording Antoine's affairs. As before, there were surprises: brown sugar? and loaf sugar? Needles, too—he had never thought of needles as items to be paid for with fur. Trousers, candles, flints, fancy garters, hats! Blankets, guns, gunpowder, musket balls, knives! These made sense, but buttons? Feathers? Calico cloth? Even looking glasses! Fishhooks—of course the natives had fishhooks of their own making.

And why was tobacco such a large item, when Indians were the ones who had first grown tobacco? Vermilion, pipes, stockings, raisins, beads, shoe buckles. *I wonder*, he thought, *how do the Natives use these things?*

The neat lists in his best writing told all the goods Antoine would be taking to his own fur post, in bales that were now made up for this, the last leg of the trip. The North canoe that would take them to their final home was loaded.

Antoine again took the bow of the *canot du nord*, Emile the stern, and he and Pretty Mouse settled themselves in the middle as they started. The canoe seemed small after the huge Montreal freighter. It felt even smaller as they skimmed beneath the rocky cliffs on one side and, on the other, the huge expanse of lake with no sight of the far shore. The water slapped and whipped against the side of their craft, but its steadiness soon quieted André's uneasiness.

The "mother of lakes" was in a kind mood, so they sped like otters. They sang much less often, their paddles keeping the rhythm almost without thought. André's mind wandered over the last days. Where, he wondered, had Basile Roche gone? He hoped never to see him again. Was he, too, searching for Denis? And how should he, himself, now go about continuing his own search? He had asked at the stockade—carefully, not showing too much anxiety lest people become too curious, or it somehow reach the ears of his enemy. But no one at Grand Portage remembered seeing such a person in recent years.

Antoine, too, had kept his promise, making quiet inquiries. He had questioned men from distant places: Lac Du Bois—what the English called the Lake of the Woods—Athabaska, the Mackenzie, even places like York Factory on Hudson's Bay. Men shook heads in regret, with a reluctant "no." Well, they had known the search would not be easy.

That, after all, was why he needed to spend a year in the wilds. Surely, in that time, somewhere, from someone, they would hear word of Denis.

He roused from his musings to find they had reached Fond du Lac, the end of the lake. Their journey again changed, as they entered the St. Louis River. Portages, too, were different—one man, not four, carried the canoe, while the others handled the goods. To André's surprise—and delight—he found that he could easily manage two bales, just as Emile did! Antoine laughed, and slapped him on the shoulder.

"Very good, my brave one! We will make a voyageur of you yet!"

Although they went upstream, the paddling was easier than in the wide rivers of the east. The portages, however, still held challenges. At the outlet of one lake, André wondered when he saw Pretty Mouse carefully winding leather cords about his legs, making his trousers snug.

"You, too, Bon-à-rien," he grunted, frowning darkly.

"But why?" André looked at his own legs.

Pretty Mouse kept winding. "You will see, Bon-à-rien. You will see."

André did see. He stepped lightly on the grassy surface—and found himself up to his knee in the soft ooze. The next step was the same. He could not avoid it—there was no dry place to step, at all. And the smell—an odor of rotting things—rose to his nostrils in a sickening wave. He pulled his leg out, to take another step, and sank to his knees again in the foul, stinking mud. Avoiding Pretty Mouse's tracks did no good; his own trail was no better. The grass swished about his legs, the steamy heat caused sweat to run into his eyes.

The merciless mosquitoes found them, and their whining and biting added to the misery. They could not free their hands to swat the insects. Clouds of black flies followed the mosquitoes and were even worse—they crawled down necks, behind ears and on foreheads, stinging fiercely.

Sweat blinded him, but he could see no place to set down his load, to wipe his face. Each lift of his foot was an effort—the swamp sucked at it, trying to hold him. When at last it let go his lifted foot was covered with black goo. If only a breeze could cool him just a little, could chase the mosquitoes, which sang about his ears! Even the small tamarack that grew in the muck offered no shade. And they would have to repeat the trip—twice.

"Sacrebleu!" he heard Pretty Mouse growl as he lifted a foot. "I have lost my moccasin! This smelly swamp has grabbed it and won't give it back!"

Pretty Mouse looked such a mixture of outrage and unbelief, Antoine and Emile laughed aloud. André felt too miserable to laugh, even when Mouse reached into the muck up to his shoulder, feeling for his lost footgear. He gritted his teeth, plodding on, step after step, unable to find a firm place for his foot, praying that he would not stumble or fall on his face. Usually a mile of portage might take two hours, but here, slogging through mud and grass, it took much longer.

When at last he put his final load down on the ridge and straightened his tired back, he stared unbelieving at the blue lake before him. Then, with a whoop of delight, he ran down the bank, tearing off his clothes as he ran. Emile was already splashing about, with Antoine even farther out, and Pretty Mouse soon joined them.

"I hate to leave this place," André told Emile, when it was time to resume their journey. The dip had given him renewed zest. "But I won't ever forget that swamp."

Within a fortnight, they came to the Mississippi—but what a disappointment. Was this puny stream the great Father of Waters? Papa had said that at Prairie du Chien one could hardly throw a stone across. How was that possible? Antoine smiled at his baffled look.

"You think this river does not look very strong," he said. "But you will see. If you were a beaver, you would like a stream like this. And we will build our post where we can find the beaver. Not here, however. We must go to where we can have the forest to ourselves."

That, it seemed, was still far away. They paddled until sundown, following the twists and bends of the river. At the falls of Pokegama they received a genial welcome at a trading post. André looked with interest at the trader's quarters. Was this what they would build? What else might the trader know?

It had been a long time, the trader said, since he had seen a white face. And no, the trader had not seen anyone who might have been Denis.

As they lay that night with the music of the falls in their ears, André wondered how many more rivers and nights before they would stop.

On they went, skimming through blue lakes and placid, rocky streams—the days still long, the sun high. Finally the day came when Antoine steered the canoe toward a bank at the fork of two rivers, where a meadow was crowned by a forested hill.

"This is it," he said. "We'll build our post here." For the last time, they unloaded the canoe. The next day, they began to fell trees.

André wished he had more practice with an ax. He tried to copy the movements of the others as they swung with precision, cutting trees, dropping them exactly where they meant. It seemed André's ax never struck the same spot twice. Pretty Mouse jeered without mercy, and Emile laughed. "Do you think you're beating rugs, to get the dust out? The idea is for the ax to bite into the same place at least twice."

André swung some more. "I'll get it yet. You'll see," he said through gritted teeth. Joseph's patience had taught him that skills came only with practice, so he chopped and chopped, even after the others had called it a day. At last his strokes fell straight and strong, cleaving the wood just as he intended.

The sawing of boards for the floor taught another lesson. He had seen this done at home: one man stood in a pit while another stood above, pulling a saw between them. But doing it was not like watching. Rolling into his blankets at nightfall, André groaned to Emile: "I always thought the one who pulled the saw upwards had the hardest job, and maybe he does, but the one in the pit—with sweat running down his back and sawdust crawling under his collar and into his eyes and making him itch—has the most misery. I'm sure glad we're finally done with that job."

Their first building was the storehouse. Not only must it shelter their trade goods—later it would house the furs they bought. He watched with growing respect while Emile and Antoine carefully notched logs to fit tightly, slanted to keep out rain.

Next, they added a small dwelling. They might need other buildings, later, but this would do for now. Last, they built a palisade, setting upright logs to surround the small cluster, with a gate that could be closed, and then their post was complete. That evening they sat around their fire in silent satisfaction—they had accomplished much on the now-shortening summer days.

Throughout the early fall, visitors came—men with stern brown faces, who spoke little. Antoine spoke with them in a language strange to André, and offered small gifts. He bought game from them, and fish. If Indians came at a time when food was ready, they joined in the meal, calmly helping themselves from the kettle. Often they picked up and examined the tools, murmuring to each other, or questioning Antoine. Emile, too, could make himself understood, and even Pretty Mouse knew the language. André was left silent, wondering what was being said.

"How did you know they would be friendly?" he wanted to know.

"They're Chippewa," Emile told him. He pronounced it Chip-away. "The woodland Indians here are of that tribe. They get along with the traders. The land belonged to the Sioux, once. But when white people came to the far eastern shores of Canada and America, each tribe pushed to the west, driving the nearest tribe out and taking their lands. When the Chippewa moved west, they fought with the Sioux to claim their lands. So now the Chippewa and the Sioux—only they call themselves Dakota—are deadly enemies."

"How could I learn some Indian words? And should I learn Chippewa and Sioux?"

Emile said he would be happy to teach André what he knew of the Chippewa tongue. "But you aren't likely to see any Sioux," he added. "Be glad of it. Some of the Sioux figure the white men caused it all—that we gave the Chippewa the guns that helped them win. The Sioux say if white men are friends of the Chippewa, then whites are their enemies.

"Here," he added, "we are deep in Chippewa country. So we needn't worry. Sioux aren't likely to come this far north. You'll see. Now that the post is ready, we'll be trading."

With so many things happening they had not noticed the days getting short. Dark came earlier, and mornings were cold, often with frost on the grass. The Moon of Flying Geese came and went, followed by the Moon of Ice on the Lakes. Now the hard winter would begin.

◈◈◈ **9** ◈◈◈

WITH A ROAR OF OUTRAGE, Pretty Mouse leaped to his feet, spilling the checkerboard and all its checkers onto the rough floor.

"You beat me! Again! Why don't I ever win?"

Emile, gathering up the scattered counters and board, grinned at him, not a bit sorry. He had made the gameboard by smoothing a piece of wood, and painstakingly carved out counters, using berries and tree bark to color the squares and checkers.

"Now you know how I feel. Antoine beats me every time. And André. That's why I like to play with you—at least I can win." The four of them spent many winter evenings at the game, in the firelight. So far, no one had beat Antoine—though he seldom played.

André looked up from the snowshoes he was almost done lacing. "I need to practice the words you taught me. Let's see. *Neet-chee*, that's 'friend,' and *Kah-too-mo*, that's 'enemy.' *Enamoring*—that's 'singing.' 'Running' is *bee-mee-but-toone*, 'jumping'—mmm—oh, that's *kwash-kwen-o-to-man*. Why, what's wrong?" for the others were laughing.

"It's the way you say it, André," Pretty Mouse said when he could stop gasping for breath. "But this time look at my lips when you say it after me," and the lesson progressed.

In his turn, André taught skills to Emile and Pretty Mouse. Emile had some schooling, so he soon learned to keep a few records. For Pretty Mouse it was all new, but after much labor he could write his name. That seemed cause for real jubilation.

"See, I can write it, see there? Paul Doyon, that's my name. Well, maybe that P is more like D. I'll do it over." And he did. He did it over and over, even on the walls of the cabin. Forming the large loopy letters gave him such pleasure they found his name scrawled all over.

They did other things, too—fencing, which the others were eager to learn, until they knocked over a pile of goods, and Antoine called a halt. Often they enjoyed singing voyageur songs, old ones as well as such new ones like "If My Top Were a Man That Could Dance" and "Hail to My Country."

One evening André remembered some sleight-of-hand tricks of Joseph's magic, and entertained them all. Antoine laughed uproariously when André pulled a long string of handkerchiefs from under Emile's shirt, all knotted together. But that was nothing to the amusement when out of Pretty Mouse's sash he drew a carrot of tobacco, and from his cap a dead mouse. Pretty Mouse had been transfixed with horror and unbelief.

"How you do that, you?" he demanded. "How you find mouse in my cap?" Several times that evening, and in later evenings, they smothered laughter as he searched and peered into his cap, as if afraid a mouse might be there again.

Evenings were not long—they went early to bed, to save their candles for the darker months ahead. Daytimes they kept busy at other jobs: spearing fish, cutting wood, feeding the dogs Antoine had bought from the Indians, melting fat to make their own pemmican and jerky.

As clerk, André recorded each day the "doings" of the post in a journal, but all too often they were humdrum. So far it seemed fur trading included much time with little trading to do. Only a few Indians had come to take "debt"—choosing goods, which they would pay for later in furs. The men waited impatiently for snow deep enough so they might use their snowshoes. Then, too, the sledges Antoine had bought needed snow for their runners to slide easily over the ground.

"Clear tomorrow," Antoine said one evening, looking out at the sunset. "Good day to practice with the dogs. Soon it will be time for Emile and André to visit the villages."

Me? Thought André, his blood leaping. He had known someone from the post would visit the Indian encampments, but he had hardly dared to dream he would be one to go.

He knew so little Chippewa, though he had listened intently while the natives spoke with Antoine! Their phrases were not like the Latin he had studied, so he listened instead for patterns and rhythms, and words like *boozhoo*, "greetings," and *mii gwech*, "thank you."

"In that case, I'm for bed," Emile said. "You'd better come, too, André, if we're to spend the day trying to do something with those wild brutes. Some of them don't want to learn to pull a sled. No wonder Indians eat their dogs—some aren't good for much else. That Petard, now—that's one cur I think I'd like to see in the pot."

"Dog's not bad eating," Antoine said with a grin. "In fact, it's good. As you will find out in a day or so." He grinned some more. "I almost wish I were going along, to watch you when you taste it. But these dogs aren't for eating—they're your transport to the Indian villages. Only, you have to train them first."

Emile groaned, and he and André exchanged a wary look. The dog Petard had been nothing but trouble. Petard (whose name André thought meant something like "firecracker") was unpredictable and not at all willing, at least when André was handling him.

He recalled bitterly the first occasion he had tried to train the animal, earlier that fall. It had been before the skunks had gone to their winter sleep, and Petard had led André right into one, as if on purpose. The stinging, horrible-smelling discharge staggered him. Eyes smarting, tears rolling down his cheeks, he was hardly able to grope his way back to the cabin. He had hoped for pity, but he soon saw there would be none.

"No, you can't come in!" they shouted, tossing out fresh clothes and bolting the door. They let him into the house only after he had scrubbed his skin nearly raw in the cold stream, and buried his reeking clothes to destroy the odor. Even then he faced snide grins, wrinkled noses and loud sniffs. He was sure the dog's face wore a malicious grin when André brought his supper. If any dog deserved to be eaten, he thought it was Petard.

Sure enough, next day was clear and sharp, with the newest snow sparkling and dry. When Emile and André went to harness the dog team, Antoine and Pretty Mouse followed. André tried to shut the door on them, without success.

"We do not need anyone to watch us," Emile said, but the others paid no attention as they settled themselves on the doorstep, to enjoy the fun. Fun for them, the boys thought with sour looks—they made all manner of unhelpful remarks while the youths struggled with the traces.

The dogs stood quiet once they were harnessed. André, who was to take first turn, gritted his teeth, planted his feet on the runners, waved the long whip, and shouted, *"Marche!"*

Nothing happened. The dogs ignored him. One, Grison, lifted a paw and sniffed it daintily.

André tried again, shaking the sledge for emphasis. *"Marche!"*

The dogs didn't move.

"Marche!" he yelled louder. This time he cracked the long whip as he had practiced. It seemed the dogs would ignore him this time, too. Impatiently he shook the sledge again. At that moment the team leaped into their collars, and André, unprepared, sat heavily on the ground. The dogs didn't stop. They careened wildly down the slope to the river. André, his feet caught in the runners, found himself bouncing across the frozen ground on his backside.

"Oww-oww-oww!" he wailed as he hit the ground with each bounce. He could hear Pretty Mouse's howls of glee and Antoine's shouts of laughter over his own yells. He staggered to his feet when the dogs mercifully stopped at the river's bank, and limped back, pants wet from cold wet snow. He glowered sourly at everyone, which did no good at all.

"Your turn," André said, not handing the harness to Emile. Wiser by having watched André, Emile kept his feet free and tossed the reins around his shoulders so his hands could grip the sledge. *"Marche!"* he cried.

79

But he fared no better. At the crack of the whip the dogs bolted, pulling Emile behind, willy-nilly. There he went, skimming over the ground in long bounds as if he were flying, his feet scarcely touching the ground at each leap. He was shaking when at last the dogs entangled themselves, and stopped.

"Hoo-hoo-hoo!" hooted Pretty Mouse. "He can fly!" It was hard to tell if he was laughing or sobbing as he wiped tears from his face.

This time I'll be ready. I won't let go of the reins, André vowed grimly as he set his teeth and took his place behind the team. *I'll keep a hold on the gangline.*

Which he did—but then when they started their mad dash he was dragged across the yard on his stomach, his face skidding through the snow.

Pretty Mouse was in the snow, too, rolling and holding his sides as he shrieked as if in agony. André looked darkly at the older men. He gathered a double-handful of slush and dumped it on Pretty Mouse's head. He felt much better as the howls subsided into giggles.

"If I were you, I think I'd swap lead dogs," Antoine said, between gusts of laughter.

"We can see that, ourselves," André muttered. He and Emile switched Ronchon into the lead spot of the traces, demoting Petard. Emile took a deep breath, rolled his eyes at André, and took his place for the next turn.

Whether it was the new leader, or that the dogs themselves were tired of the game, or perhaps even that the trainers had become more wary, things went better after that. Nevertheless, when the farce stopped that evening Emile had a bloody nose and scraped cheek, and every bone in André's body felt sore. Neither felt kindly toward the grinning dogs, nor the grinning Mouse and Antoine, either.

"To think," Emile growled, "that when I was little, I wanted a dog for a pet. Now I would rather have a man-eating tiger." And André agreed.

Next day matters went better, and by degrees the dogs became more manageable. They still snapped at each other, and the boys soon learned not to get too close to their sharp teeth. As for Petard, he could not really be trusted at all. However, they learned to control the team and take them romping happily down the trail. The trip to the Indian villages would really be possible.

When the day came, they loaded the sledge with care. Antoine was sending gifts—tobacco, needles, cloth, and other items the tribes prized—to encourage trading. Dressed warmly, and with snowshoes, the boys started for the camp of Lame Hawk, thirty miles away. Theirs was a serious errand, as well they knew, but a holiday feeling lightened their steps. Their first trading venture!

André's questions burst out when they stopped for their first rest. "It's strange to tell the Indians we're here. They know it already."

Emile eyed him pityingly. "Of course they know. They probably knew we were coming, while we were on our way—they have ways of finding things out, and passing on news.

"But this is different, my friend. Now we make a formal announcement: 'Here we are. We are friends, ready to trade—come.' And of course the Big Chief Antoine does not go—he is too important to go knocking on doors around the country. He sends his slaves—us, Bon-à-rien."

"I wonder why Antoine let me, when Mouse speaks so much more Chippewa."

"But you won't need to do any talking. All you need to do is watch, and listen." Emile said. "And perhaps you'll learn something you want to know."

André thought for a moment. "But—will it be all right to ask about my brother?"

Emile did not answer at once. At last, he said, "We have to see, first, how friendly they are. How open. You cannot rush in with these things, André. With Native people, you must allow time." He sighed. "But, if they like us, and if they feel like talking—and we can't be sure of either one—then I will ask. I promise."

André thought this over for some time before he went on. "I know Antoine has been asking around, trying to learn about my brother, to help me. But I think he was helping me in other ways, isn't it true? On the way here, I mean. In the canoe." He thought back to the times he had felt protected, even the fact that he was here at all.

Emile gave him a sidelong look. "You mean, did he keep the men from giving you trouble, and try to make things a little easier to start? Perhaps. Not by showing you any favors himself. But he told Pretty Mouse to watch over you. I think the others knew he wouldn't let anyone bully any other—because it all makes for a better brigade."

So he had been coddled. André's face burned. *I was so proud to think I was a true voyageur, but all the time I really was still a good-for-nothing.*

"It wasn't needed after the first," Emile smiled. "You showed that you would give your best—you were a good voyageur. You always pulled your weight and carried what you could. And after Grand Portage—well! All were proud of you there.

"It was not for you—it was for your father. Antoine would do anything for him. Joseph saved his life, and Antoine does not forget. If it is in his power, he will find your brother." He bent to untie the dogs from the small tree, and they went on.

Lame Hawk's village seemed like a small town. Several large lodges filled a clearing. From one of them came a hunter who had visited their post. "*Boozhoo*," he greeted them, unsmiling, then led them to a lodge, and made hand signs for them to be seated.

At once a stout woman and a young girl brought food. Antoine had warned them they must eat, hungry or not, what they were offered, so they did—and found it a delicious stew. After the meal, Emile and the hunter spoke, and though André listened hard and understood few familiar words, he had a sense of the exchange. He thought Emile explained that they were ready to trade, and offered that the men of the village could take "debt" from them, to be repaid in furs.

He could not tell what answer they gave, before a man escorted them to another lodge. Here, again, they were fed, after which Emile spoke. At another lodge, another meal followed. And another speech. Now André was beginning to see the pattern.

"I'm getting full," Emile whispered, and André's stomach felt tight, too. Then they were led to the lodge of Lame Hawk himself.

The chief received them with friendship. André felt pride in Emile, who smoked with ceremonious courtesy, and spoke with dignity. He noticed that Lame Hawk looked at the ground when Emile spoke, the way Antoine had told them was proper. Having heard Emile's speech before, André knew what it was about. And he heard more words he understood.

Meanwhile he studied the chief. He was a tall man, sturdy, with no touch of white in his hair, and a sober face that wore a kind look.

Emile stopped, waiting for Lame Hawk's reply. It was slow in coming. By watching the chief's hands and listening to his tone, André found more meaning in the strange words.

Lame Hawk knew, he said, that the trader Antoine was his brother who would deal fairly with the tribe. But his young warriors had tasted firewater and wanted it. And he knew Antoine (whom he called The Open Face) would not give it to them. He waved aside Emile's explanation that Antoine thought whiskey was "bad medicine." That, he said, was true. It made the young men wild, so they did very bad things, but they craved it anyway. A trader to the south would give it, but he was much farther off, and less generous. Lame Hawk would talk to his young men, but he could not keep them from the other trader. He sounded truly sorry.

A long pause followed. Then Emile began a roundabout speech about other white traders, their ways, their looks, and, finally, their different kinds of hair, sometimes black like the Indian's own locks, or lighter. Of course such hair as André's was most unusual—a man with such hair was seldom seen.

A man with such hair? Lame Hawk lifted André's hair in his hands, studying it. He looked into the distance. Perhaps. He did not know. He had not seen for himself. But he had heard—how long ago?—of such a thing, a man with bright hair. Perhaps it was not true. Perhaps it was only women's talk. He could not say.

André could hardly contain himself. He kept his face rigid and stared at the fire while Emile carefully, without any show of anxiety, continued to probe. Lame Hawk thought someone had said a man with such hair was in the lodges of Makwa, the Bear.

André bit his lips hard and kept still, though he felt his hands tremble—Makwa was chief of one of the bands Antoine planned them to visit later! Yes, he was quite sure that was the place, if that was what Lame Hawk had said.

Somehow he sat quietly during the long talk. He could hardly wait to get to their own lodge before he burst out, "Makwa's village! Did I hear that right? Emile—only think! What if that should be my brother, Denis? Oh, do you think we could go to Makwa's village right away?"

Emile was stern. "Easy, André. This is not something to do in a hurry. There are things here we don't know. And you can't rush Indians—they think through a plan and take their time. Let's go back to the post. Antoine will know what we should do."

"Right," André said slowly. "It's wiser, I know. And we don't have enough trade goods anymore today. But if it should be Denis—it's hard to wait."

Though the dogs ran fleetly, the thirty-mile return trip seemed endless to André. Antoine listened thoughtfully to their recital. He put his hand on André's shoulder.

"No one has told us about this man before. It's as if it is a secret. If it is Denis, perhaps he is hiding. There must be a reason why no one talks openly of him. You must not let it be seen that this is very important."

He thought for a moment. "You should go first to a few other camps. They may have heard you have asked about the fair

man, but if you say no more about it, they will not become
alarmed. But be careful, André. To show too much interest in this
person may put him in danger. I seem to remember—Runs When
He Walks once traveled far away with others to bring back the
stone for a peacepipe for his tribe. He too might have heard of
Denis. Visit others, then go to him, then Makwa."

And André understood. He and Emile brought gifts to
several encampments, not saying a word about a fair-haired man.

Runs When He Walks, when they reached his village,
proved to be a younger man than Lame Hawk. He seemed
friendly, almost jovial, and fond of Emile, wanting to keep him at
the village long after the time they planned to leave.

Without prodding, he spoke openly about the man with
hair like corn. Yes, he had heard of the man. He had come to
Makwa's band—oh, many years now. Three times the loons had
come and gone since he had first heard of him, and the man had
been with them many winters before. But, no, Runs When He
Walks had not seen him, not ever. Nor had many others seen him.

"I have heard they are very careful of him," Runs When
He Walks added. "They guard him closely. Perhaps it is because
he brings them good luck. While he stays with them, their hunts
are good. Their people stay strong. They do not wish to lose him.
That is what I have heard."

André swallowed, though his mouth felt dry. *Keep your
mouth shut,* he reminded himself. *Pretend you don't care.* Emile's
warning look reminded him to show no feeling, but his heart
plummeted. If the man were watched so closely, how could they
ever get word to him about the news from France? His spirits were
low as they returned to the post.

André's dejected air and dragging feet got no sympathy from Antoine.

"Ho," he said, grinning at André's long face. "You give up too easily, Bon-à-rien. What we will do now, is this. You and Emile will take presents to Makwa. This time you must stay many days. Make friends with his young men. Join in their games—running, shooting. Show them how you can make 'talking leaves'—that is what they call writing. Be a friend.

"It would help if you were as strong as they are. If they see you can shoot and run as well as they, you will gain their respect. Maybe even their admiration. And, if they like and admire you, who knows? They may want to help you."

André's despair vanished. He knew it was a good plan. Even if they did not find Denis there, it was wise to win Makwa's friendship. As to the games—well, he was not the fastest runner, but Emile could run like the wind. And he would practice with the bow and arrow, but he was already good with a slingshot.

For several days André and Emile practiced running and shooting, skills he knew the tribes prized. Emile was already fleet, and André could almost catch him. When his arrows fell short of the mark time after time, he groaned, but he kept at it until he felt he could make a respectable showing. Since Antoine was putting aside his own business in order to help his search, it would be up to him to make best use of the chance.

At last, he and Emile were off, with loaded sledge and hopeful hearts, headed for Makwa's village.

◇◇◇ 10 ◇◇◇

THE VILLAGE OF MAKWA'S BAND was large, and widely spread. Surprisingly, almost the first lodge into which they were invited was that of the chief himself. He welcomed them with dignity, standing straight before his fire. He wore a red coat glittering with gold braid—the coat of a British army officer! A big, sturdy man, they could see why his name was Makwa, the Bear.

It was a good start, and they should have felt easy. And yet . . .

"They do not like us," Emile whispered that night. "They suspect us. I think they have heard something about our search. Perhaps they fear we are here to steal their 'good luck.'"

"I know," André had felt it, too. Oh, outwardly they were treated as friends. They were lodged with the chief's son, Crow Man, who spoke to Emile as if he were a brother. His son Makes Thunder was André's age, and the two went about the camp together. André thought Makes Thunder truly liked him, though he seemed reserved.

Often they were followed by Makes Thunder's small sister, Little Berry. When he made "talking leaves," sending one to Emile to ask him to grab his nose, she giggled in delight—but then, when she made talking leaves of her own, why did they not work? She showed him favors, bringing him the Indian sugar made from maple trees, a squirrel tail, an odd rock. André's hair she treated as something very odd. She peered at his head, to see if it grew that way out of his scalp. She felt of it, and tugged at it to see if it would come out. Emile thought this hilarious, if a bit scary.

"Have a care, André. Perhaps they will want to keep you, too, for good luck. Or maybe just your scalp." But André could not laugh. Still, they seemed to wish him no harm.

More than once he bit his tongue to keep from asking an awkward question. "I can see Antoine's advice was good—they treat us like we belonged here." He spoke softly, as they prepared to sleep. "Did you hear all those admiring murmurs when you beat them in the running game?"

Emile rolled over on the blanket. "You didn't do so bad, either, with the bow and arrow. That bull's-eye was a pretty shot."

"That was just luck," André confessed. "But it made me feel mighty good. But, Emile, I haven't seen anything of a man with fair hair. No one has mentioned such a person. I can't help wondering if there is one in the camp."

Emile sighed. "Easy, easy, André. Give it a couple more days. Maybe it was all a wild tale, but, who knows? Maybe something will turn up."

Late the next evening, a group returned from a hunt. André had spent the day with Makes Thunder, hunting small game with his slingshot, and joined Emile in their tent after sundown. He could tell Emile had news, but, until the women who served their food had left, they did not speak.

Then Emile whispered, "He is in the lodge third from the end, near the old birch." Every muscle in André's body went stiff. He caught his breath.

"But, I must warn you, " Emile said, "It won't be easy. I think he has a wife and child. And he may be watched."

André thought hard. "Somehow, I have to talk to Denis, and tell him everything. We can't just 'steal' him—he has to be willing to come. He's been here a long time. What if he's a prisoner? If we try to help him escape, they'll be after us sure. And what about his family? Emile, this is dangerous for all of us—you and I, and Antoine and Pretty Mouse, too. We can't make any mistake. What do you think we should do?"

"We can take them all with us, if we must. The woman and child could go on the sledge. We three must run alongside. But it must be soon, André—before they find we know about him. Tonight, after everyone sleeps."

André's whole body was cold with excitement. "As soon as it's quiet, I'll slip over to his lodge. I'll have to explain about France, and our plan. And I'll help him crawl out, and then we'll run for it." He stood up. "I'll feed the dogs, now, so they'll be ready to run. And if nobody's about, I'll get the sledge ready."

Goose bumps covered his arms as he made the preparations for their flight, but his mind stayed clear and steady. He felt like a sneak and spy, to be repaying the kindness they had received with such a deed.

But if Denis was a prisoner, perhaps there was no other way. What, he wondered, would Makwa do? Certainly he would pursue them—could they outrun him? With luck, they would have a head start before Denis's absence was discovered. Still, the Indians surely would not keep him against his will—that would not bring "good luck."

They waited until the village was quiet. Then they waited some more. Not even a dog was snuffling when André felt it safe to slip out of the lodge. The sliver of moon was behind a cloud, hiding his approach. Inch by inch, listening, he crawled and slithered from one dark patch to another. At last he reached the lodge where his brother lay.

He looked about cautiously, but nothing stirred. Then, dropping to his belly, he crawled to the door flap, lifted it carefully, and slid in. In the dimness he saw three blanketed humps, all sound asleep. He reached the largest, and placed his hand over the man's mouth.

"Denis, Denis! Wake up!" he whispered.

The man in the blanket growled something in Chippewa, and sat up, his hair gleaming palely in the light of the fire's embers. He shook his head, and looked at André, grunting in surprise.

"Shh! Listen! I'm your brother, André. I came here to look for you. I have news."

"Hunh?"

"Shh—quiet! Denis, listen to me. I'm your brother. Joseph and Berthe sent me to find you. There's been a letter, from France. You are to go there, to our grandfather. So you must come with me now."

The man seemed befuddled with sleep. "What are you saying?"

André's whisper became urgent. "Our grandfather in France needs you. You are the next *comte*. I have come to get you, to take you home. Everything's ready—but we must hurry! Quick, before the tribe wakes up!"

To his relief the man seemed to rouse. He untangled himself from his blanket and stirred up the fire. By its light André got his first look at the man who was his brother.

Yellow hair hung to his shoulders, and his chin bore blond whiskers. He seemed big, with stooping shoulders. André had not expected his brother to look so old—but perhaps the hard life had aged him. He waited tensely—what would Denis say?

His words, when they came, were halting. "I do not . . . understand. But . . . I have . . . not so good . . . the French. Can you speak the Chippewa . . . or English? Do you say . . . is it you are brother to me?"

"Yes, yes! I'm André—don't you remember? Think of France, and the ship, and Joseph! But we must get you away from here, and quickly! We can't wait, or it will be too late. We must get you to France before Basile Roche can do you harm!"

The name Basile Roche seemed to evoke some feeling in his brother.

"Basile Roche? Is he . . . Why do you think . . . ?"

"I'll explain later—there's no time now. It's just that he wants the estates that should be yours. But please, please, let's go!"

Still the man did not move. He swore softly. "Basile Roche, hmm? He is . . . a weasel, or worse. He lies, he cheats, he steals . . . And he kills. More than once . . . he's killed. He killed . . . Rabbit Man and . . . his woman Yellow Cloud . . . burned them up . . . in their winter lodge. To steal their furs. And a trader, too . . . what was his name? I forget. For his furs. Just to get his furs."

His voice dropped. "And worse! His heart . . . is stone."

"But Denis, we must hurry! We have to leave right now, if we are to get to the post before Makwa misses you. Let's go," André hissed.

"Softly, softly, boy." The words came slowly. "There is . . . something here . . . I don't know. But it is not . . . right. Fifteen winters . . . fifteen winters or more, I have been with Makwa. My home . . . it is Boston. I have never . . . been to France. I'm not . . . your brother."

Not his brother! André sat back on his heels, breathless.

The man went on. "My name . . . it is Joshua Small. Do you speak the Chippewa? Or the English? I speak them better than the French."

He had come, he said many years earlier, from his home in Boston. He had started as a *coureur des bois*, but the life had been too hard, too dangerous. Once he had come with Makwa's band on one of their hunts, and they had been very successful. They believed he brought them good fortune, like a good-luck charm. So he had remained with them, and now was one of the tribe. He had a wife and son. He would never want to leave.

André said, "But they do not feel sure of you, do they? They did not want us to know you were here. They hide you from other white men."

"They do not hide me. It is I who don't wish other white men to see me," Small said. "They often have bad names for men who choose to live the native way. But I have become one of them. They want me to stay. Tomorrow I will go to the council, and tell them that I feel no kinship for you. I am a man of the Chippewa."

Confused and troubled, André somehow made his way back to Emile. Even relating the story didn't make it seem real.

"He's not my brother—he's the wrong person, he is Joshua Small. He couldn't even speak French! So I haven't found Denis after all.

"But, Emile, he spoke of Basile Roche, terrible things, and I'm scared. It sounds as if he's not far away. What if he's learned the news from France, too, and is hunting Denis, just as I am, and finds him first? He is a killer, Joshua Small says."

Emile spoke comfortingly. "But Roche doesn't know you, or that you are searching. And, don't forget, you are with Antoine Felix. Even such a man as Basile Roche must have a care around Antoine Felix."

That was true, and André felt better. Still, it had been a bitter disappointment. He shook his head. "We'll have to start all over again. Now what?"

"That's easy." Emile rolled over into his blankets. "We'll just stay another day, to show them we've no designs on their good-luck man. But it wasn't wasted, André. We made friends, and they'll trade at our post now. That's important. And, some other way, we will find your brother."

But André's hopes were dimmed. Even watching Joshua Small the next day, as he appeared to the council, made him no happier. Seen in the daylight Small was lanky, stooped and unkempt. His shirt was greasy, his beard scraggly and he seemed dull.

Emile murmured, "I would not want him for your brother, André," and André agreed.

That day their young friends held a hunt, which the boys joined. Even without Small, they had success. Emile's shot secured a deer, which was strung on poles to be carried back to the camp. Makes Thunder lifted one end to his shoulders. André, who took the other, suddenly stepped into a hole and turned his ankle. With a stout stick to lean on, he could hobble a little faster. Their progress with the deer was slow, and they soon lagged far behind the rest of the party.

As they made their way through a thicket, a noise of crashing startled them. Suddenly, in front of Makes Thunder, a she-bear appeared. She, too, was startled, and reared to her full height with a deep growl, claws outstretched.

They had no time to be surprised that the late winter days had brought a bear out of her den. Frozen in their tracks, they stared at the animal as she stared at them. Makes Thunder, within her reach, stood rooted to the spot by the poles he carried—he could not retreat or defend himself.

But André at the other end could move, and he had a stick. Dropping the poles from his shoulder, he leaped forward as he had at Grand Portage.

"*En garde!*" he shouted, though the words were wasted on the bear. With all his force he lunged at the bear, driving the staff into her middle. With a startled "woof!" she dropped to all fours, and loped off into the brush.

The boys stared at each other in awed silence for a moment.

"You have saved my life," Makes Thunder said solemnly. "So now my life is one with yours. From now on you are my father's son, my brother." Crow Man, when he heard the story, with an almost invisible smile, put both hands on his shoulders in friendship.

Emile grinned widely. "Antoine will be dancing in thanks to you, too—this band will be our friends for life."

Next day they returned to the post with happy news—
Makwa's band would bring their furs to Antoine. But, André
added grumpily, they had failed to find Denis.

Antoine looked at André, head hanging, kicking morosely
at the sled runners. Then he whacked him on the back with force
that nearly knocked him to his knees. "André! You give up too
easily!"

Pretty Mouse spoke. "You know, André, there have been
traders on these waters for more years than I can count. A white face
is not that new to them. The only white men they speak of are those
who are special—like your good-luck man. So it is too soon to stop
asking. Only, you must ask the right people. The ones who know."

Antoine nodded. "Pretty Mouse, you amaze me with that
brain hidden in your brushy head."

"A little one, maybe," Pretty Mouse said modestly.

"The Mouse has said it," Antoine said. "Ask in the right
places. And the right place would be where many traders bring
furs, and talk about all sorts of things. But there is not much
time—you see how the days are getting longer. Soon the ice melts,
and we must head for Grand Portage, and then home. Before then,
we have much to do—we must press our furs into bales, the
accounts must be ready. So we must act fast.

"If we hurry, one more trip can be made. I hope that we
find your brother. If not, we will try again at Grand Portage. Or
I will take you with me next year. This quiet search may take more
than one year. We will not give up, that I promise."

The work at the post had to be done, as André well knew.
He must keep his part of the bargain. Still, his heart sank. Wait
another year?

Records kept him busy. Nearly every day, Indians came with thick furs, to pay their "debt." They brought other goods, too—pemmican, Indian sugar, wild rice (which they called wild oats). As days lengthened they began the many preparations needed to start for Grand Portage when the ice and snow should give up its grip on the land. A surprising number of Indian bands came to offer friendship—next year's trading should go even better.

One day, Makwa's band came, Makes Thunder with them.

He acted strangely unhappy, trading his furs hesitantly. Still, he remained at the post when others of the band left. He ran the dogs with them, he ate Pretty Mouse's stews, he watched as André wrote, he curled in his blanket on the floor to sleep—but said nothing of what troubled him. Words that needed to come out seemed locked in his brain.

Antoine said one night, "These warm days are when we may see a bear come out of his den." At the word "bear," Makes Thunder tossed an anguished look at André, folded his blanket about him, and left the building.

Speechless with surprise, the others in the room looked wide-eyed at one another. Then André followed his friend. Makes Thunder was standing not far away, shoulders hunched, brooding by the stream's edge. "Is anything the matter?"

Makes Thunder looked at the ground. "My heart is bad. You saved me from the bear. You are my brother. You have been a good friend to me. But I have been a bad friend to you."

André protested. "But that's not so! Why, we're the best of friends. I know I'm leaving, but I'll be back. We'll see each other again."

Makes Thunder held up a hand to silence him. "I am ashamed," he said sadly. "I have known that you search for a brother. Our people said your brother had bright hair like you. You looked for him in our village. You asked other villages about him. When you could not find him, you looked sad."

André said nothing. He knew, by now, that Indians took their time to speak, and that something serious took a very long time. Makes Thunder's message must be very important indeed. He shifted his feet, waiting, but Makes Thunder seemed to find it hard to find words.

"I have kept silent, when I might have spoken. I feared my brother André would find another brother, and I would lose him. So I said nothing of what I had remembered about a bright-haired man. For a long time I have done this bad thing."

He took a deep breath.

"But my brother saved my life. How can I hide from him what I know? That is why I am ashamed."

André could wait no longer. "Do you mean—have you some idea where my brother—my *other* brother—might be?"

Makes Thunder nodded, but it was several moments before he spoke. "Years ago, I journeyed with my father and some from another tribe. Three times the geese have come and gone, since that day. We went to the place of soft red stone, the place where we make peace pipes. It is in the land of the Dakota, the ones you call Sioux. They are our enemies, but all tribes are safe where the stone of peace is found."

André took a deep breath, holding himself silent, while his blood rioted through his veins. *Hurry, hurry!* He wanted to say. *What do you know? Tell me!*

"Men of other tribes were at the place of red stone. One man was called Sun Walking. His hair shone in the sun, like yours.

He had white eyes with blue sky in them, like some Mandans. But he was not with Mandans. I think he came with Assiniboines, or Lakotas, maybe. I saw him one time, but my father Crow Man did not see him, nor others we were with. So I have not always been sure of this—was it a vision or real?"

Can this really be true? Is there news of his brother at last? André took a deep breath. He spoke slowly, not wanting to be disappointed again. "Do you mean Sun Walking might have been my brother?"

"That is what I think. Crow Man said I must tell you this. And more, that another is seeking him. This other has promised much whiskey and beads for his scalp." He looked anxiously at André. "He would perhaps pay well for your scalp, too. Of course you are safe with our people—a scalp means nothing if it is not claimed in battle."

In the wave of delight that washed over him, André grabbed Makes Thunder in a crushing hug. "Oh, thank you, thank you! Oh, Makes Thunder, I am so glad to hear this! I must tell Antoine!"

Antoine, when he heard, spoke warningly.

"He does not know which tribe, you say. I wish it were the Mandans—they would be easy to approach. The Dakota are not our friends. To go among them could cost your life. And there is that other seeker, who wants only a scalp. André, we must think about this."

But they did not just think. Antoine sent couriers with questions—men who traveled fast, carrying nothing but news.

Every day André waited, trying not to hope, as the messengers returned. Each time his heart would leap eagerly, only to fall like a stone when there was nothing . . . nothing. It seemed every inquiry brought nothing but failure. And time was slipping away.

I can't just think about my problem, he reminded himself. *I'm here to keep records.* So he made himself keep busy with the lists of furs they had taken and packed, to have all in readiness when they started for Grand Portage at the end of the season:

43 buckskins, large
85 buckskins, small
164 beavers
12 good bears
11 otters
19 muskrats

And so on. Everything was listed. All would be in order when they had to leave.

There was something he didn't want to think about—how could he tell Joseph that he had failed?

But then express news came back from Charles Chaboillez on the Red River, so exciting he could not control his eagerness. The report said that only this year such a man had been reported among the Dakotas. It seemed likely he was there still.

"Go soon," Antoine urged. "Before long, the Dakota will start their spring buffalo hunt. André, I will send you to Charles Chaboillez, and ask him to help you. He is again in this country, not so far. But you must go alone—Emile and Pretty Mouse are needed here."

Makes Thunder spoke. "I will go with my friend."

Antoine shook his head. "To go to Chaboillez with André would be good. But, my friend, a Chippewa cannot safely go to the Dakota. Start tomorrow, André, you have not much time. When the ice leaves, we start for Grand Portage. You must be back by then—we cannot wait."

André's heart sang with renewed hope. A chance, at last! Oh, surely this was the right one, the lucky one! A small scared pang underlay his joy. There were so many ifs! Was it his brother? What would happen with the warlike Dakota? He must make the attempt—but how would it end? And would he be in time?

◇◇◇ 11 ◇◇◇

DAWN WAS YET FAR OFF when Makes Thunder shook André awake.

"We must go," he said. "I smell a storm in the air, and I do not like the sky."

Groaning, André rolled out of his warm blankets, and hurried to harness the dogs. He saw nothing odd about the sky—only a small cloud that his hand could hide. Still, Makes Thunder set a fast pace, and presently there was a screaming wind that struck fiercely. Their faces stung from the dry snow it flung at them. Their arms and legs grew stiff as the cold searched under their *capotes*. They hunched into their woolen coats and plodded on, heads down, into the teeth of the storm.

More snow came, whirled on the wind, hiding the trail and fighting their every step. The world was eerily dark. Stinging pellets driven by the icy wind hunted out every opening in their clothes, finding their cheeks and noses. Their breath froze into icicles as they struggled against the fierce blast. Its frigid fingers tore at their coats, reached down their necks to chill their backs, slid icily up their arms, through their middles, so that they shivered constantly. At nightfall Makes Thunder stopped near a thicket of spruce, whose lower branches swept the snow.

"We camp here, " he said. Crawling under the spreading branches, he dug a space in the snow. Here the wind did not reach them, and a small fire lessened the chill as they huddled in their blankets, the dogs near. Somehow they slept.

When dawn came, they went on, fighting the same cruel wind. Snow powdered their clothes, making them like ghosts. André felt frost on his eyebrows and lashes, and his knees stiffened like stumps. Still, though ice seemed to reach his bones, inside he burned with excitement. At last he might find Denis. Nothing else mattered, nothing at all.

When they finally sighted Chaboillez's fort, André's face felt so stiff he could not even smile. He had not expected so huge a store: it was more than three times the size of Antoine's. The house, too, held many rooms. He thought it resembled a castle. About it were dwellings for his men, with a long house André knew must be for his voyageurs. All was surrounded by a stockade of pointed poles that formed the hallmark of a fur post.

André remembered their meeting at Michilimackinac. As did Chaboillez, who asked of Antoine, of their trading, of André's work as clerk.

Yes, Chaboillez would help—though, mind, he did not promise success. The tale of the bright-haired man might be only a story, with no truth. Still, they would soon know.

"I will send you in a *cariole*," he said, "to Jean-Baptiste Cournoyer. His post is near the Lake that Talks. If the brother you seek is with the bands that trade with Cournoyer, he will tell you.

But your friend cannot go with you. It is the country of the Santee Sioux."

"I will go with my brother. I am not afraid," Makes Thunder said quietly.

Chaboillez's face was stern. "You are brave, my friend. But—it would not be wise. The Santee will not be pleased to see you in their lands. You would be in danger, and that would put your friend in danger. No, I will send a man from here."

André had to swallow a large lump in his throat when it was time to say goodbye to Makes Thunder. But they made their farewells like true Indian brothers, not even touching each other, though their eyes showed their sadness as they wished one another good days ahead.

The next day the *cariole*—a sledge with a back, so one could sit and ride—waited, with fresh dogs, a dark-faced man beside them. He spoke very little, but seemed tireless on the trail.

André didn't want to talk. Thoughts of the problems that lay before them chased themselves around in his mind. *What if they could not find the man? What if he turned out to be someone else, like Joshua Small? Perhaps he, too, would choose to remain with his Indian friends—what then?* The journey itself was filled with uncertainties, too. They might be delayed by storms, or bands might have moved to their spring hunting grounds. And time was short— Antoine had pledges to keep. Could he wait, if they were late? But he must stop such thoughts.

He reminded himself of Emile's parting words.

"André, I have been thinking. Why don't you and I come back again next year? I would like that—should we, André?" The thought lifted his heart, and made him smile. Only the presence of his austere guide stopped him from capering a bit with the joy of it all.

Jean-Baptiste Cournoyer's post was larger than Antoine's, with more men. André saw a mixture of Indians, *Métis*—men with French and Indian blood—and Canadians. Joseph Charette, who served as an interpreter, welcomed André into his home.

He had forgotten how comfortable it felt to be in a family. Charette himself was a burly, cheerful man, and his stout wife seemed equally happy. The pretty eldest daughter, Marie-Thérèse, brought him tea, and took his torn shirt to be mended.

Three smaller children eddied around him with games and questions. "Was it true wolves could talk?" "Had he ever been in a bear's den?" Their chatter ceased only at supper, when their father began to speak.

"There is such a man as you seek," he said. "This I know, for I have seen him. He lives in the village of Silent Wolf. Where he came from before that, I cannot say. For three years now he has lodged with the chief's family. The band values him for his courage, his skill and his wise counsel. But, I must warn you, he may not be the right one. There are often white men living with the tribes."

André knew that. He reminded himself of Joshua Small.

"Not all are good men. Sometimes they've done some terrible thing and must hide. Such a person is dangerous. He may harm others to keep himself safe."

This was a new idea. André's spoonful of pudding paused halfway to his mouth. "We don't want such men here—who could trust them? They cheat, or lie, or worse. Because of them, Indians think all white men must be cheats and liars. This man we speak of may be such a one, and not your brother at all. Or he may be wanted back east as a lawbreaker."

He shot a quick, stern look at his daughter. Marie-Thérèse gazed demurely at her moccasins, wearing a small secret smile.

What is that about? André wondered. He put it into his memory to puzzle over later.

Charette went on. "We will visit Silent Wolf, and see what we can learn. You must prepare yourself for whatever we may find."

André swallowed hard, looking at his plate. Was he to face another disappointment?

"Perhaps alarming you is wrong. I want only to prepare you for trouble. You see, lately I have heard whispers of something that makes my hair stand on end."

He looked hard at André before continuing, in a serious voice: "First the Chippewa, now the Dakota also are murmuring of a *windigo*."

A *windigo?* What did that mean? Not knowing what to say, André said nothing.

"Do you know what a *windigo* is? It is a man who has become a devil. Chippewas think one who is truly evil turns into an ogre. We would say, a cannibal. They believe such a man has lost all human feeling, is capable of any brutal deed. He kills without mercy and even eats his victims. And now I hear fearful stories of such a creature, stories I have not heard in many years."

Chills ran up and down André's back at the heavy menace of Charette's words. "You do not mean—you do not think my brother is this *windigo?*"

"No, no, I'm sure he is not." Charette shook his head. He looked at his pretty daughter, who was listening hard, giving her a comforting smile. "But he is the one the *windigo* stalks. In the tepees they say the *windigo* hates or fears this man. Perhaps he has known him before. Perhaps he is afraid of the man's medicine. He

has tried to kill him already. Indians will protect him if they can—
but a *windigo* has unusual, almost magical powers. They fear the
windigo would destroy them, in horrible ways. Just the thought of
it fills them with dread."

André thought for a moment of his own frightening
encounters—the rocky rapids, the wild storms on the big lakes,
the lynx, which he had thought was a *loup-garou*. Whether real or
imagined, each struck him with a paralyzing terror. And then,
somehow, it became a thing of the past. How had that happened?

Charette got to his feet, filling his pipe. "I do not wish to
frighten you—but you needed to know. Now I must make plans,
so we can leave tomorrow at first light."

We! That must mean that Charette would go with him.
André tried to stammer his thanks. The interpreter waved them
aside as he left the room.

"We go to find a man—two men: your brother and this
windigo. I do not believe in *windigoes*, but this idea is growing
among the Dakota. If someone claims to be one, his plans are vile.
He disturbs the peace of the land. For the good of all, we must rid
ourselves of anyone so wicked. I believe that the Indians cannot
do it, their fear of his power is too great, so that is my job. Now,
I must find men to go with us."

Left with the family, André tried to be a good guest. The
little Charettes wanted him to play, but troubled thoughts of his
brother and the *windigo* intruded.

He was surprised when, shortly thereafter, Charette
beckoned him into a room where a council fire burned. Several
Indians, wrapped in blankets, stood straight and still in the
dimness. Their height and slenderness, different from the broader
Chippewa, marked them as Dakota.

Proud, dignified, they listened to Charette deliver a long, flowery speech. André could understand only parts, but enough to catch something about the great bravery of the Dakota, their prowess in battle, their skill in hunting. André's skin tingled as he spoke of a young white man, their brother Sun Walking, who hunted with them, living in the village of Silent Wolf. And here, he said, was Sun Walking's brother, seeking him, having lost him many moons ago. Would these friends now bring Sun Walking's brother to him?

A long silence followed. André looked at the faces, which showed no expression, at the fire as it burned and snapped, and at the tall shadows of the warriors. If only they would speak.

Finally, gazing off in the distance, one brave replied. He knew of Sun Walking. But a dream had come to him that told him not to go.

Charette remarked that any who helped in the search would gain rewards. But the next speaker also said, regretfully, that he could not go. It was time to prepare for the buffalo hunt.

A third brave only shook his head.

Charette's next speech included the word *windigo,* which André recognized and then of "women's talk." Was the interpreter suggesting their fear of the cannibal-spirit?

This the Indian spokesman denied, vehemently. But he went on, earnestly declaring that the *windigo* was not just women's talk. This one had done dreadful things already. He had killed men, with his bare hands, to get their furs. He had burned a hunter and his family in their tepee. Now he pursued Sun Walking.

But he, Ghost Wind, was not afraid. Nor did his friends have fear. They could not go to the village of Silent Wolf because they had no musket balls.

The words circled round and round.

It's the windigo, not the musket balls or visions, André wanted to shout. *You don't want to meet up with the windigo. No one does.* But of course he must not say such a thing, even if he had known the right Sioux words. Despair made his heart sink. If the Indians would not guide them beyond Lac Qui Parle, what would they do? How else could they be sure of being safe, and welcomed like peaceful friends? To proceed alone would be perilous. There must be some way to lighten this fear, to see it another way, but how?

He saw frustration on Charette's face.

Suddenly André had an idea. Maybe—just maybe—there was something he could do. He stepped in front of Ghost Wind. Staring into the brave's eyes, rocking back and forth on his heels, he began to chant. He got louder and louder, waving his arms, muttering sounds. "O-wah-goo-she-mah-wog-bo-tee-sha-vee-lo-rop-so-goo!" he chanted.

Ghost Wind looked hard, amazed and puzzled. Was the white man crazy?

"Ooo-ka-woo-ka-hocus-pocus-abacadabara-foo-bam!" André gabbled. He spun around, shaking his fingers in Ghost Wind's face. And then—he reached into Ghost Wind's hair—and drew out a musket ball.

Ghost Wind's eyes popped. A chorus of astounded murmurs came from the men. They stared, dazed.

André whirled about, uttered more gibberish, and out came another musket ball from a brave's belt. And here was a third one, plucked out of the ear of Spotted Bird. Musket balls seemed to come from nowhere. They watched, open-mouthed, as other surprising things appeared in odd places—a feather in

Leaper's blanket, a handkerchief in River Bear's pouch, a small cake, such as had been served for supper, in Old Moon's shirt. They looked in dismay at the places these things appeared, puzzled. Their faces showed it was a serious matter.

As he pulled a handkerchief from Cloud Man's arrow quiver, he could feel the mood change. Mystified as they were, the Indians knew here was a spirit beyond what they had seen before. If this power could find musket balls in ears, could it do other things as well? It would be worth studying. Perhaps it was the equal of the *windigo*.

Charette, too, felt the change of atmosphere. He used this chance and spoke warmly.

"You see, my friends, if musket balls are needed, they will be there. But we go as friends. We do not need weapons to visit friends. We need only someone to help us find the right trails."

Now there was no shortage of men willing to go. In the end, Ghost Wind and two others were chosen. Ghost Wind held his head proudly, pleased with the honor, but was it not his right? After all, had not the first musket ball been found in his hair?

They set out on the journey at dawn.

As they drew closer to Silent Wolf's camp the next day, other worries nagged André. There seemed to be something Charette was not telling him. Did he have secret knowledge about the man they sought? Did he have reason to think it was not Denis at all? Or had he fears of the dangers before them? André's own fears mounted. Not knowing what might happen kept him anxious.

Most of all, the *windigo* haunted him: who, or what, might it be? Was it a jealous medicine man? Who else might hate Denis? How many enemies, indeed, must they escape before Denis was safe?

◈◈◈ **12** ◈◈◈

SILENT WOLF CAME HIMSELF to greet them as they approached his camp late that afternoon. Plainly, he felt friendship for Charette, Ghost Wind, and others of the party. He listened to Charette's long flowery speech patiently, though André could hardly wait for it to be over. At the end, the chief nodded, speaking slowly.

Yes, Sun Walking was here. But Silent Wolf's heart was sad. He was no longer the same Sun Walking. He walked now at the edge of the spirit land.

In the silence that followed André heard himself gulp, as he waited for Silent Wolf's explanation.

Did Charette know about the *windigo?* He had come into their lands two moons ago, building a shack near the Lake That Talks. He was cruel, greedy, merciless. Silent Wolf's people were much afraid. This *windigo* had terrible powers. Men who did not bring him their furs disappeared. He cheated those who traded with him. But no one could resist him. It was not safe to defy him. After the *windigo* heard of Sun Walking, he wanted his scalp.

But Sun Walking laughed at the *windigo*. He said the stories were just to frighten people. He said the man did not have any magic, he was not a *windigo* at all, only a very monstrous man.

One day Sun Walking and Yellow Hawk had gone hunting. It was a good hunt, and they secured game. On their way home, the *windigo* caught them. He shot at them, and hit Yellow Hawk in the leg, so that he fell.

Then he came at the two with his knife. They had no more musket balls, so Sun Walking ran at him, and wrestled with him. They struggled over the knife. When Yellow Hawk managed to get up and lunge toward them, the *windigo* fled.

But the *windigo* had stabbed Sun Walking many times with his knife. Sun Walking's life's blood poured out onto the snow. He lay now in Silent Wolf's lodge, but his spirit was almost gone from him. No one knew where the *windigo* had gone—perhaps he was near, waiting to pounce, even now.

In André's mind, things he had heard came together so that all at once the picture was clear before him. He broke in excitedly:

"What does he look like, this *windigo?* Does he have black hair, like Monsieur Charette? Has he a scar on his face, from his eye to his chin? And does he walk as if he rolled from side to side, like this?" To show them, despite his lack of words, André traced a line across his own face where the scar would be, and walked with a roll.

Silent Wolf stared. "Is it that you have seen the evil one, then?"

"Yes!" André almost shouted. "He is called Basile Roche!" Rapidly he told what he had learned—that other tribes also

112

believed Roche a murderer and thief, that he pretended to be a *windigo* to frighten hunters into trading with him.

As he explained why Roche wanted to kill Denis, Charette nodded. It seemed to answer a question in his mind.

Silent Wolf led them to his lodge. There, on a buffalo robe beside the fire, lay a man with hair that gleamed like André's own. His face was red with fever, his breath came feebly in shallow gasps, and his eyes stayed closed.

André fell on his knees beside the pallet. It was Denis, he knew. It was not only the hair, like his own. Joseph had spoken of a scar on his arm, and there it was. And there was the mark like a strawberry under his ear that Joseph had described.

The chief's voice was heavy with real grief. "There are deep knife wounds, three of them. And his head has been hit. Somehow he drove away the evil one, but he was hurt badly. Our medicine man does all he can, but I do not think his spirit will be with us long."

No! André's heart rebelled. He had not come so far, and found his brother after such troubles, to lose him now. He reached for the limp hand under the deerskin robe.

"Denis! Denis, do you know me? I am André, your brother."

The figure in the robes did not move. Silent Wolf put his hand on André's shoulder. "He is stronger than this morning. Perhaps he will come back. We will hope."

Charette reached out to André. "Come. Let's let him rest. We can come back later."

But André was not ready to leave. He leaned against the buffalo robes, listening to his brother's ragged breathing, humming a lullaby Maman had sung to him, holding his hand. The medicine man stopped by the fire to brew a potion of dogwood and willow bark, administered with rattles and charms.

Dogwood and willow bark—the herbs Maman said helped reduce fever and pain! He hoped it would help Denis now.

Indeed, it worked. Later, so soft he hardly heard it, a slight moan stirred the pallid lips. He waited, hardly breathing. The eyes blinked, once, then again. Nothing stirred for some time.

André sat, waiting, as hours passed, humming now and again, saying prayers. Women came to tend him.

Then the blue eyes opened to look at him unseeing, closed, and opened again as if really waking. And Denis spoke.

"What . . . are you . . ." His voice came as a mere thread of a whisper.

"Hush! I'm André, your brother. Don't talk now. I'll tell you everything when you're stronger." He had hardly spoken when Denis' eyes closed again, and he slept.

The medicine man knew his business. In a short time he returned with a sort of broth, which he fed to his patient from a horn. He put damp deerskins on his head, murmuring in his strange language all the while. Presently Denis began to breathe more deeply and evenly. André's grateful sigh was a prayer of thanksgiving.

In the morning, Denis showed more improvement. He was awake longer. He began to turn his head, raise his hands and lift his shoulders from the bed. Strength came back, so that, though he slept often, he wanted to talk. André poured out his story again and again, as Denis fingered his miniature of their mother.

"I remember her—do you? No, you were newly born. She was so very gentle. But our father—our grandfather—"

André shook his head. No clear picture of any part of their life in France came to him.

114

"I will go back to France, as they ask," Denis said. "I love our grandfather. He was stern, but kind and honorable. So I must return, to help him with the people of Arseneau. It is *noblesse oblige*—if you are born a noble, it is your duty to help those less fortunate." He smiled at André.

"But I will miss my life with my Dakota friends. What about you? You, too, have tasted the joys of living in the wilderness. Will you, too, return to France?"

André's tongue stumbled. He had enjoyed the adventures of the past year. He would like to be with his new-found brother, if only it was possible. But the life in France would be strange to him, and he had no wish to go there. For him, happiness was the life of a voyageur and the trader.

"I can no longer be a warrior here, or a voyageur. I must go home and become a *comte*," Denis said, smiling. "But one thing I will change. When I go, I hope to bring with me a lady to be my countess. If she will go. Do you think she will? You have seen her—Charette's daughter, Marie-Thérèse."

Marie-Thérèse! Now it all fell into place in André's mind. That was the key to the exchange between Charette and his daughter. The brothers gazed at each other in delight. He guessed that Denis had now spoken with Charette about the future, for Charette had acted pleased, and Denis wore a look of happiness.

But time was short. They must leave while there was still snow for the passage of the *cariole,* for Denis could not go on his own power. He sat in the *cariole,* bundled in robes. The others took their places, with Silent Wolf and Ghost Wind in the lead. André's pack was light, after giving the things in his "possibles" bag as gifts.

His heart was light, too, so that he wanted to sing, even though there was nagging fear.

The warriors looked warily about as they made their way down trails overhung with trees. André, too, kept an anxious lookout—Basile Roche was still somewhere out there. Maybe he would lie in wait for them at Grand Portage? Whatever damage Denis had done to him in their fight would have healed by now. Would they ever be safe?

Silent Wolf said nothing, but André saw that he led them by roundabout trails, slower but safer than the way they'd come.

The rivers they traversed were no longer solidly frozen, with large stretches of fast open water and lacy fringes of ice along their edges. Snow along the banks allowed swift passage for the *cariole.* André relaxed. From now until they reached the Cournoyer fort, the river on one side would protect them. He looked at Denis, gazing at the scene—was he sad at leaving his Dakota friends, or eager to see Marie-Thérèse?

The noise of the river was getting louder. Were they nearing a falls? He wanted to ask, but no one else was speaking. The rumble of the tumbling water had reached them for some time. Judging by the thunderous roar, they would soon see the cataract, a great waterfall.

Ghost Wind led the way along a narrow track beside the river, with Charette at his heels. Silent Wolf kept close to the *cariole,* making sure it did not tip on the uneven ground, while André brought up the rear. As they made their way among the trees that overhung the bank, with the river's thunder becoming ever louder, he strained for a closer look. Suddenly the magnificent cataract was before them.

The majestic falls stopped them in their tracks, and they gazed in awestruck silence. Cascades of water foamed over a rocky shelf, and poured in a golden thundering torrent that drowned their voices, holding them in wonder.

All at once something catapulted out of the trees, shoving the *cariole* toward the water. It tumbled, over and over, down the bank.

Denis shouted as he rolled out. Before he had gained his feet, a bulky figure pounced upon him, knife upraised. Basile Roche! No! It mustn't happen!

André leaped toward them as he saw Denis's hand reach up to grab the arm holding the knife—if only he were closer—his wounded brother would be no match for Basile.

Silent Wolf moved like a whirlwind before him. What happened in the next moments André could not see—the chief's body hid the struggle, which was over in seconds.

André heard a growl, then a cry of rage and fear—and the body of Roche hurtled down the bank, plunging with a splash into the tossing angry flood. Once, his head surfaced, mouth open in an unheard scream, only to disappear under the seething torrent.

The dark bundle, like rags, went tumbling on down the stream. It bobbed to the surface one short moment far downstream, then was gone. They did not see it again.

The watchers on the bank stared in stunned silence. They saw no further sign of the man in the clutches of the water.

Silent Wolf turned away with a grunt.

"That was the *windigo*," Ghost Wind said. "He is gone."

"He is gone. I have finished the *windigo*. It is good," Silent Wolf said. "He did much evil, frightening my people. With his bare hands he killed, and with my bare hands I have rid the world of him."

He started down the trail, and the others followed.

They traveled well into the dark. Next morning, Silent Wolf and Ghost Wind said their farewells. Tears shone in Denis's eyes as they placed their hands on his shoulders, and pressed his cheeks with their own.

No one spoke as the three travelers went on their way, reaching the fort of Cournoyer that evening. Now, at last, the somber mood, which had hung over them since meeting Roche, lifted.

All was gaiety as Denis and Marie-Thérèse were married, and prepared to start their new life. Uppermost in André's mind was the time slipping past—he wanted to say, *hurry, hurry! Antoine is waiting!* Or would Antoine and the others have left?

Luck was with them. They reached the post in good time. There outside the palisade of pointed poles stood Antoine, Emile, and Pretty Mouse, with broad smiles. Before André could signal the dogs to stop, they pulled him from the *cariole*, thumping him on the back and shaking his hand. Emile grinned from ear to ear. Pretty Mouse grabbed him around the middle and whirled about with him. And then they looked at André's "guests"—Denis and Marie-Thérèse.

"You did it, Bon-à-rien, I knew it! I knew you would! Oh, Bon-à-rien, you did it!"

At a sudden snort from Antoine, they all turned to look at him in surprise.

"Enough of that!" he said, frowning at them with fierce determination. "That's not his right name—it never was! He deserves better. Call him Quevillon, or just plain André, or whatever he likes. But not that. You hear me?"

André looked at him gratefully. "Didier," he said. "I want my name to be André Didier. There's no other name I'd rather have." No matter what title he had been born to, he truly belonged to the Papa and Maman who had cared for him all his life.

Now they turned to hand Marie-Thérèse out of the *cariole*, and Denis, who was now able to help himself.

Almost at once they began the chores to wind up their trading season. As André finished the records for Antoine, he kept thinking, *It won't be long, now. Papa and Maman will be so pleased to see Denis. Too bad he will leave so soon—but now we will get other letters. And won't they be relieved about Basile Roche! They can speak and live freely too. This bully has gone from all our lives.*

Then it was time to return to Grand Portage, for the start of their homeward journey. As their heavily laden *canot du nord* slipped through the shining waters, André cast a last, almost sad, look at the small post they left behind, just before a bend in the river hid it from sight.

Their paddles shone in the sun with the rhythm of lift and dip, lift and dip. The canoe skimmed through clear waters, through forests just now awakening from their winter sleep.

At Grand Portage, André would buy the gifts he'd planned. Then would come the adventure of crossing the lakes, and he could paddle stroke-for-stroke with his mates, he knew. Then they would be home! Joseph and Berthe would be excited to see Denis! And how they would delight in Marie-Thérèse. All would be merriment, until they sailed off for France.

But that would not be the end, oh, no. He was not Bon-à-rien anymore, he was André Didier, a true voyageur, with a plume in his hat and a swagger in his walk. Life was golden.

His heart lifted. "Sing!" he shouted, and as the voices rang out, he bent to his paddle.